THE

RINGDOVE.

A ROMANCE.

LONDON:

PUBLISHED BY G. PURKESS, COMPTON STREET, SOHO.

PREFACE.

————

THE following "eventful history" is founded upon occurrences which have actually taken place since the commencement of hostilities between Mexico and the United States. It is perhaps fortunate for the novelist that "the course of true love never did run smooth," for otherwise he must perforce have resorted to his imagination for incidents, instead of finding them ready made to his hand, or occurring, as they do every day, under his own immediate observation.

The author has represented an interesting phase of the passion of love, in making Louis Dumont bear all the galling insults of Robert Rosal, with a stoicism that could only be inspired by the master feeling; love for the sister enables him to support the annoyances of the brother, and at the same time to persevere in a course of kind offices which in the end have the effect of conquering the most prejudiced ill-will. In the youthful, impassioned and enthusiastic Benita, we have exhibited the force of natural affection, which displays itself towards her brother while their relationship is still unknown, and she is unable to account for the feelings which agitate her mind.

Much has been said recently against the national reputation of the Mexicans for valour; but though they have in most instances been vanguished by the superior discipline and determination of the American troops, there are many brave men in the Mexican army and navy who do no discredit to the most courageous people on earth; and the author has endeavoured to depict such an one in Captain Mejia, who knew how to treat an adversary with respect, and shrank from no danger which he had a chance of fighting his way through. Many instances have been related of vessels eluding the blockade of Vera Cruz, in a manner quite as surprising as the manœuvre of the Mexican captain.

It was necessary to state this by way of explanation, for in these latter days of criticism, readers have become philosophers, and not only require a moral in every tale, but that the incidents shall be entirely probable and accounted for by the most natural reasoning.

London, January, 1848.

THE RINGDOVE.

ROBERT ROSAL INTERRUPTS THE INTERVIEW BETWEEN HIS SISTER AND DUMONT.

CHAPTER I.

THE LAKE AND THE MAIDEN.

The moon had been an hour above the horizon. The broad bosom of Lake Borgne reflected its brilliant light without a ripple upon its limpid surface. The dark shores around girded the lake like a belt. There was not a cloud on the star-freckled sky nor a shadow upon the silvery wave. All was silence, too, save now and then was heard the shrill shriek of the eagle from his eyrie on the shore, or the splash of the awkward alligator as he plunged affrighted into the flood.

There is a nigh spectator of this night scene. It is a fair young girl who has left a villa half buried in the grove by the water side, and of which the moon light, shining bright upon its portico, gives a faint glimpse. She has reached th verge of a low, jutting cliff, upon which two or three large oaks are growing, and casting beneath, upon the green sward, a shadow almost black; yet where the slender moonbeams make their way through the leaves, they fall brilliantly upon ground, and look as if myriads of glow-worms had been scattered upon the sward.

Upon this little eminence she stands, gazing intently upon the wide, bright, still lake. Its silence seems to have a charm for her and to speak to her soul, for she has been long standing here, gazing now at the waters as they reflected the sky, and now at the azure sky; and now again she would listen to the shriek of the eagle, as it broke upon the night, and to the heavy startling plunge of the alligator near by, with feelings akin to awe. But her eyes were most intent upon the lake, stretching far off over its waters as if expecting to behold some object make its appearance. When her eyes could distinguish nothing, she would bend forward in an attitude of listening attentively, frequently bending her ear low as if to catch the faintest sound that might be upon the water.

The maiden was Isabel Rosal, the heroine of our story.

She was in her nineteenth summer, tall and graceful, yet not too tall, for her height gave her dignity. Her complexion was Arabian, dark and rich olive, warmed with the blood of a generous clime. Her dark eyes were sparkling and full of soul and feeling. Her features were strikingly beautiful, and expressive of a generous and proud spirit. With all the softness and fascination of her sex, she possessed resolution and firmness of character in an unusual degree.

She was the daughter of an opulent Louisianian, who had distinguished himself at the battle of New Orleans, and subsequently retired to his estate, on the shores of Lake Borgne, a few leagues from the city of New Orleans, there, in the retirement which he coveted, to enjoy the honours he had entwined about his brow, and to educate a beloved son and daughter. But circumstances, which will be unfolded in the course of this narrative, interposed to destroy these plans of happiness. Suffice it to say that Isabel Rosal, and Robert Rosal her brother, were orphans, their mother only now being alive, and residing upon the estate on the lake, in the possession of a princely fortune, to which the two children were the only heirs.

Isabel had left the villa just as the moon rose, and bent her steps to the cliff where we find her watching the opposite outlet of the lake; for the lake communicated with the Gulf of Mexico in the south eastern direction from the place where she stood.

'It is ten o'clock. The tide flows and will soon turn! He should have been in sight—in the middle of the lake by this time!' she said, after steadily watching the faint, far off outline of the horizon. She spoke with an air of disappointment and impatience combined. She walked for a few moments quickly up and down the sward, beneath the shadow of the old trees that overhung the cliff; and then again keenly bent her gaze in the direction of the outlet of the lake. After looking for several moments, she turned away with an air of vexation.

'Why should I expect him without a wind to waft him along? In my impatience I thought only of the flowing tide, and forgot that he must have a breeze to fill his sails. The lake is as calm as a sea of polished silver. He will not come to night! Hark! What is that I hear? It is the sound of oars on the right along the shore. I cannot be mistaken!'

She stepped forward a little and after waiitng a moment saw distinctly a small boat gliding along close under the bank and pulling swiftly but cautiously towards the cliff where she stood.

Surprised but not alarmed at this discovery she wrapped closer about her form the dark mantle which she wore, so as to conceal her white dress, which might have betrayed her presence, and then, sheltered by one of the trees, she watched the advance of the boat. It contained but one person, who was rowing. As he came near the cliff he rose in his boat, and using one of the oars as a paddle, guided the skiff into the land and leaped ashore. The place where he landed was perfectly dark, being overhung by the cliff, so that if he had been her brother she could have hardly made out his person. Yet there was evidently an instinctive recognition of the stranger in her heart, for it bounded and throbbed tumultuously from the moment she saw him rise u in the boat. But as he wore a short cloak and a low cap which concealed his features, and was some twenty feet beneath the place where she stood,j shej dared not give utterance to the name that was upon her lips.

The young man, for such his general air and movements betrayed him, having hastily secured the boat, took a sword from the seat and buckled it beneath his cloak. He then looked up as if in search of the steep path that ascended the cliff. As he lifted his face a luminous moonbeam fell upon it, and revealed for an instant the handsome features of a young man of four and twenty, with a bold, frank air, and a countenance agreeable and prepossessing. His cap, too, displayed a gold band and button, which betrayed his profession to be that of a sailor. Upon seeing his face, the maiden clasped her hands together with joyful surprise, and was about to spring forward with an exclamation and the name Louis on her lips, when, as if prompted by a secret impulse, she drew back and smilingly restraining her emotons, she said,

"I will see what he will do."

With this pretty purpose she kept the tree between her and the stranger, as he mounted the path to ascend to the top of the cliff. From this spot a gravelled walk led along a ridge towards the barn of the villa, a walk shaded by trees, and such a one as lovers delight to ramble in when the moonlight weaves from shadows a carpet of fantastic figures beneath their feet.

When getting to the top of the cliff he paused and looked around. He turned towards the lake and after keenly looking in the direction of its outlet, he said,

"There is no probability of seeing the cutter up to night. The wind is gone to sleep for the next twelve hours. Now for my dear Isabel. I trust she has not followed the example of the Zephyrs and gone to sleep too. It is now three nights since I promised to be here ; and I can't expect she will keep watch for me to the last !"

"Yet I have done so, sir laggard," exclaimed Isabel, suddenly appearing before his surprised vision.

"Isabel!" he cried joyfully, and bounding towards her, he clasped her to his heart,

"Noble and true girl," he said, as he held her back a moment at arm's length and gazed with all a lover's admiration into her dark eyes, "how good you are to be here! I was just about forming a plan to communicate with you ; for I expected that not seeing me last night nor the night before you would not look for me to-night, and be in your room. It is so like you to be here !"

"Then don't be surprised. Truth to tell, Louis, I was just about going away when I caught the sound of your oars. Pray how is it you come in a boat and in this way ? Where is your vessel?"

"Outside at anchor, some five leagues away."

"Why did you not come before? You wrote me from New Orleans eight days ago that I might expect you at eight o'clock at the latest last Thursday night! And here you have just made your appearance. You do not deserve that I should have been here in waiting for you. Give me a good account of your delay, and, perhaps, I will forgive you. There is no offence more grievous than for a true lover to disappoint his mistress !"

"I confess it, Isabel. I will now defend myself," he said in the same playful tone in which she had spoken. "When I sent word from you to the city that I should be here on Thursday, I did not anticipate that I should be prevented by orders from a source that I dare not disobey without forfeiting my commission ; and though it is but a commission in the revenue service it is my all and my profession !"

"Do not speak so disparagingly of the service you are in, Louis. It is not, it is true, so desirable as the naval, but it is honourable. During the war the revenue cutters behaved gallantly, made numerous captures, and performed a number of very brilliant achievements, which have reflected glory upon the navy of which they were an acting-branch. I will not hear you speak lightly of your profession!"

"I must be content with it, and so you love me no less, Isabel, I am satisfied with it, or ought to be. Besides I am looking up, as you shall hear."

"What were these orders you received, which prevented you fulfilling your intention of coming here so soon as you expected ?"

"They were from the Secretary of the Treasury. They reached me the very day I despatched the note to you, but an hour after it was sent. The orders informed me that there was an armed schooner which had been cruizing for several weeks in the neighbourhood of Cape St. Antonio and the Tortugas, under the Mexican flag, and which had boarded and plundered several vessels ; and that, as she was a very fast sailer, I was forthwith to sail in pursuit of her and use every effort to capture or destroy her. You may judge that such an order, relieving me from the tedium of coast duty, and opening before me the excietment of the chase and a brush with a privateer, gave me no little pleasure."

"Are you going on this dangerous service, Louis ?" she asked with emotion, all her womanly fears awakened at the idea of the danger to which her lover would be exposed.

"Yes, Isabel. It is a service of honour. You are the last person to dissuade me from it, I well know. You are silent—but I know you will never bid me stay at home ; I should be unworthy of your love, if love for you would make me indifferent to dishonour. I had no sooner got this order than I prepared to get my little cutter ready for the new service she was destined to enter upon. I shipped twenty-five more brave men, added to the eight six pounders a long eighteen, which I placed just abaft the foremast, took on board powder, ball and small arms, and left the port the second day after receiving my orders. This accounts for a part of the delay ; and for the rest, I have been all the afternoon becalmed off the entrance to the lake."

"And were you going on your perilous cruise, Louis," she said reproachfully, "without informing me ?"

"No love. I despatched Tilly to inform you that I was suddenly ordered off, and should probably be absent a month."

"I have not seen him."

"Because the black rogue would not go. He took my letter and pretended to start, but came back secretly and concealed himself on board till I had got a dozen leagues down the river. He then made his appearance, and pleaded as an excuse his wish to go with me and see some fighting. So when I found that you would be left in a state of uncertainty and anxiety, Isabel, I resolved to keep it with the coast and run in to see you for an hour or two and say ' good bye ;' which would not put me more than three or four hours out of my time. But just as I got off the entrance to the lake there fell a dead calm. As night approached, seeing no prospect of a wind, I took my lightest boat and four men, and pulled into he lake. The tide set us towards the western shore, aed landing near the Spanish fisherman's hut, half a mile from this, I left my men there to rest, after their long row, and drink Manuel's sour wine, and alone pulled hither to seek an interview with you. —Happy was I to find you here watching for me. Now you have heard my defence. Am I pardoned, fair Isabel ?" he said, smiling.

CHAPTER II.

THE TWO SONS.

THE maiden did not for a moment make any reply. She was too much distressed at the prospect of being so shortly seperated from Louis, perhaps, considering the dangerous service he was sent upon, perchance for ever.

"Do not speak so lightly, Louis. Do not ask me to forgive, when there is nothing to pardon. I am grieved at the intelligence you bring to me. Is it indeed true that you are sent in pursuit of this formidable Mexican Privateer, and in your small vessel too. You can never capture her; but on the contrary, will be taken yourself."

"Do not fear, Isabel. I have the utmost confidence in my cutter's crew, and in less than ten days I hope to give a good account of the enemy."

"Well, Louis, go! I will not detain you. Go where duty calls you. But I would you had rather staid where danger was less."

"And the life inglorious, Isabel," he said, with animation. "No, no! I no sooner read the orders from the department, than I felt like another man!"

"And did you not think of me?"

"Yes, but only with the proud consciousness that I was now about to be placed in a way of rendering myself more worthy of your love Isabel. I did not so much think of your regret at having me go away, as of your pride in my success."

"And I will think only of your success, Louis; I will pray for it. If you would let me, I would go with you."

"Much as I should love to have you with me, Isabel, I would not expose you to the dangers and inconveniences of the sea; no, not even, if you would consent this very hour to become my bride, that you might honorably accompany me. I shall probably be absent less than a fortnight. On my return we will be married!"

"Neither then, nor ever, shall Louis Dumont be the husband of Isabel Rosal!" cried a fierce voice close by them.

"My brother!" shrieked Isabel, rushing to place herself between Robert Rosal and her lover.

"Draw Dumont, and defend yourself!" cried Robert Rosal, putting his sister aside, and advancing towards Louis with his sword drawn.

"Robert, hold!" cried Isabel catching the shining blade in her naked grasp. "What madness is this?"

"Do not interfere, Isabel, or I will not be answerable for the consequences," exclaimed the young man, who had approached the spot where they had been conversing unperceived, and been some moments a listener. He was dressed in a light grey undress naval jacket, buff sportsman's open trowsers, and wore upon his head a broad palmetto hat. About his waist was a belt, in which was worn a short sword. The sword he had drawn, and with it was now advancing upon the lover.

Louis stood calmly and unmoved, till he heard him menace his sister, when he said sternly—

"Dare to harm that lady, Robert Rosal, and you shall answer for it to me. What quarrel have you with me that you thus come upon me like a robber?"

"Quarrel? None. I will have none with the son of a murderer! It is vengeance I seek! I heard that you sought the hand of my sister. I was with the army at the Rio Grande, when the news came to me. I did not delay an hour. Just as I was, for I was hunting near the camp when the message came to me, I started homeward. I arrived to-night at my home. I sought my sister in her chamber. It was vacant. A servant had seen her walk towards the cliff. Here I have found her and in your presence. Is it not enough, sir, that we are foes by nature, that you should seek to win the love of my sister. No deeper insult than this could you offer me. Draw, Louis Dumont! I am here to avenge my father's blood."

"Robert, I did not slay your father."

"Nay, brother, why call the son into judgment for the father's act?" cried his sister.

"Away, ingrate! Do you dare speak in his defence. But what more can I expect from one who is so far forgetful of herself as to receive the attentions of the son of the man who slew her own father? Speak not, Isabel, or I shall be tempted to punish your treachery to your own honour and mine, by plunging my sword into your heart? Stand aside? You will not? Louis Dumont, if you are a man, follow me. We will settle our little matter where there are no women to interfere. I have for years forborne to avenge my father's death upon you, as I ought to have done. Nay, I have outwardly been courteous to you; but when you have presumed upon my forbearance, to address my sister, the daughter of the father whose life your father basely took, it is time that I should interfere. Follow me to a more retired part of the lake shore. We will see which wields the best sword."

"Louis, I forbid you to obey him!" cried Isabel, seeing the young officer about to move, as if to comply with his hostile invitation. Robert, are you lost to all affection for me, all consideration for my presence, that you act thus?"

"You have forfeited my love, Isabel. Do you pretend to be ignorant that Col. Dumont, the father of your revenue lover here, killed your father and my own?"

"No, brother, alas! I would it were otherwise But it was an honourable duel!"

"No, only the semblance of an honourable duel. My father was run through the heart after having been twice wounded and disabled in the sword arm. He would not ask quarter, and the base assassin passed his sword through his body!"

"Do not recur to this dreadful event, Robert. It has been talked of by you till I am heart-sick of it!"

"It is false, Robert Rosal! My father slew him in honourable and fair combat. The aggrievance my father had was a heavy one, and the terms of the unhappy contest were, as I myself have seen them on record, that they should fight till one cried for 'quarter!' This your father refused to do, and he died by the laws of the battle. Were it not for the love I bear thy sister and her presence here, I would prove to thee presently with my sword, that my father slew his enemy honourably."

"Thou liest! He assassinated him. It was one of the foulest deeds that ever stained the hand of a murderer!"

"This to me! I pray thee, fair Isabel, retire, and let your brother and I settle the dispute on the spot. I can bear no more, even for thy sake!"

"And what if thou dost slay Robert? Think'st thou, Louis, I will ever give thee my hand or forgive thee? No!"

"Fear her not, Louis!" cried Robert tauntingly; "if she will forgive the son the father's deed, she will forgive thee for thine own, even if thy victim be her brother. So let us to work. The hilt of my sword grows hot in my hand!" and he made a menacing step towards the lover.

Louis threw himself into an attitude of defence, when Isabel, with a sudden spring, caught her brother's sword from his hand and threw it into the water.

"Now, Louis, to thy boat, and speed thee away quickly, if you ever hope to have favour in my eyes more. It is my brother whom you would combat with. For my sake forgive his words and hasten from the spot."

"For thy sake I will avoid the rencontre, Isabel!" responded Louis, hastly pressing her hand to his lips. "Farewell! Ere long we shall meet again, when I hope you will confer on me the authority of your protector."

"God preserve and return you to me in safety!" she answered with tears.

The next moment he had sprung down the cliff and was in his boat shoving off from the shore.

Robert was not idle the meanwhile. No sooner had he found himself deprived of his weapon in so extraordinary a manner, than he threw himself from the bank and plunged into the shoal water where he saw it disappear. He recovered it and came out of the lake with deep curses against his sister and her lover, when he saw the boat containing Lewis shoot out of the shadow on the other side of the bank.

"Coward and son of an assassin! You do well to fly the vengeance of the offspring of a murdered man. If your feet ever again tread these shores you die, and the ungrateful girl also who dares to love where she should hate!"

Louis made no reply. He slowly rowed away along the shadowy shores of the lake until he was lost to the sight of the infuriated and disappointed young man. Robert stood for a moment looking after him, and then, turning away, ascended rapidly to the top of the jutting bank where he had left Isabel. He expected that she would have flown in terror from him; but he found her standing, calm and unmoved, the moonlight streaming between the branches above her head, fell upon her person, and revealing her features with their resolute expression. He advanced angrily towards her, and presented his sword to her bosom. She did not stir; she simply said,

"Coward, to menace a woman!"

"But you have aggravated me, Isabel," he responded, instantly dropping the point of his sword to her feet." You have deceived me. How is it that you have shown any favour to this Louis Dumont, whose father murdered ours?"

"The act of the father should not be visited upon the son, Robert. Besides, you are in error—it was a duel!"

"It was not; it was, a foul murder; the whole world called it so at the time."

"Even if it were, Louis Dumont is not a murderer! He has none of his father's guilt. He is acknowledged everywhere and by all to be a young gentleman of the most upright character, amiable and brave! You know him, however, as well as I do, and have no need that I should speak in his praise!"

"Which I see you are nothing loth to do. I treated him with courtesy when he used to live on the farm near us! but it was from pride, lest the world should say I was revengeful. Beside, he was a neighbour, and we often met unavoidably. But since he has been in the revenue service, and I have thought more and learned more about my father's death, I have hated him. Judge, then, my indignant amazement when I learned, at Point Isabel, where my vessel was, that it was rumored that you were about to be married to him!"

"How did you hear of this, brother?"

"I hardly know how the news got there. I was on shore that day on a hunting party with some of the officers, and it was spoken of as we were taking our dinner under some trees on the edge of the chapperal. The same night I was on my way hither to see if there was any foundation for such a rumour. Judge what my feelings must have been when I found you here billing and cooing by moonlight. Isabel, you have done what I cannot easily forgive. When did you see this Dumont to love him?"

"I will answer you as plainly as you have put the question, brother. I have loved him from childhood. We grew up together as it were; you being away at school, saw him but seldom and knew little of it, for when it began to assume, as years increased upon us, a tender form, I concealed it; and the more especially when I found that you had a strong prejudice against him. But I have never known the time when I did not love him!"

"And all this time you knew he was the assassin of your father! You are not worthy to be my sister. Hark you, Isabel! This young man—this murderer's son—has now escaped me—avoided me, too, on a plea that makes me still more deeply his enemy—his love for you. But I solemnly swear that if he comes near you again, or you favor him in the least, he shall die by my hand."

"So, out of your holy hatred for the murderer's son, you would become one yourself. This is consistency."

"Consistency it may not be; but it is the resolution by which I shall be governed."

"I do not fear that you will ever so far forget yourself, Robert, as to be guilty of an act so base as you speak of.—With all your hatred, Louis, you are still a gentleman. You possess high-toned sentiments of honor, and would scorn to degrade your name by an act so criminal. I do not fear for the life of Louis at your hands! You are too noble to harm him!"

"You are right. I will not kill him and do a murder; but he shall meet me when next he comes ashore from this cruise, in honorable conflict. He cannot refuse to give me an opportunity to avenge my father."

"With my consent you two, born to be friends and brothers by congeniality of disposition and similarity of character, shall never meet. Oh, if you could meet him as a friend, Robert, how happy you would make both him and me. Believe me, he honours and loves you."

"For thy sake!" sarcastically answered the young man, as, thrusting his sword into his belt, he rapidly walked before her to the villa.

CHAPTER III.

THE OLD SMUGGLER.

LOUIS DUMONT, after being lost to the eyes of the incensed brother of Isabel, pulled along the lake shore until he came, at the expiration of a quarter of an hour to the inlet of a small creek. This was an inlet that led by a winding w y to several fine plantations in the interior.—Its mouth was overgrown by huge trees which cast it into the darkest shadow. Some of the depending branches nearly touched the water, and so completely concealed the entrance that one unacquainted with it and not noticing the outward flow of a current, would pass it even in the day-light without discovering it. To those who were familiar with it, it was known by the denser grouping of the trees thereabouts.

Upon coming opposite the mouth, Louis, after being sure of the entrance, pulled his boat directly under a heavily drooping branch, and after passing a few yards under the thick canopy of foliage which compelled him to stoop low as he glided beneath, he found himself in a bright opening out the stream and in the full moonlight. On the bank, which was cleared for a few yards of trees, stood a low cabin, constructed of poles and withes interwoven and surrounded by a rude gallery in the Spanish fashion. On the shore were drawn up two or three small pirogues, and a few feet from the hut was anchord one of those broad short luggers, with one stump mast and with open decks, used by the Spanish fishermen of the lake. This, with the boots upturned upon the strand, the hut and its picturesque gallery with the tall dark forest around, formed a fine moonlight picture. To complete it and give it life, the lofty figure of Manuel the fisherman was seen standing near his door upon his long gun.

"Who goes there?" he called just as Louis discovered him.

"Un amigo, Manuel. Are my men with you? Tell them to bear a hand. There is a cloud rising away in the south-west which will give us a wind before mid-watch."

"Won't your excellency please to come ashore and take a glass of my vino," said Manuel in a hearty, hospitable tone, as Louis drove the bow of his boat against the sand.

"Yes, thanks to you, Manuel, I will; for your wine is far-famed!"

"It comes from my brother in Oporto, who every year sends me a cask, senor capitan?"

"Your brother is a Portuguese then. I thought you were a Spaniard, Manuel?"

"May not a Spaniard live in Portugal, senor. Be sure my wine is good whence ever it comes!"

'There are people Manuel, that do say it has never paid excise duty. But of course this is slander," said Louis, smiling as he stepped on shore.

"Bien! When you can find me at smuggling wine, senor, you are at liberty to seize it. You can't expect me to pay duty on a present from my brother!"

"If I saw such a cask of wine coming on shore, I fear I should have to put the excise mark on it, Manuel. But till then I will drink your health in what I find in your hut."

"It is not good manners, capitan, for a guest to ask his host where and how he gets his vino. If thy conscience will not let thee drink, say so. I'll warrant thy fellows here within, have no such misgivings."

Louis smiled and entered the hut. He well knew the old man was a suspected smuggler; for the carrying on of which business his location was admirably chosen, as a boat communication was possible all the way through to New Orleans. For his own part he had no doubt that annually many scores of casks

THE FATAL DUEL BETWEEN THE FATHERS OF DUMONT AND ROSAL.

of wine had found their way, transferred from vessels in the lake, past Manuel's door, to the city, free of any duty save that which was exacted by Manuel for his countenance and assistance. But as he had never been detected in this suspected contraband trade, he had been suffered to remain there, though closely watched, and at times receiving visits quite unexpectedly. He was, therefore, well known to Louis, who, while he well knew him to be a smuggler, so long as he could not catch him at his deeds, let him remain without molestation, and frequently visited at his hut in a friendly way.

No. 2.

Manuel, on his part, while he kept on good terms with the numerous officers, was very cautious and wary, and took very good care that they should never find him engaged in any other occupation than his ostensible one, of fishing.

Recently, within a few days of the period when the order came to Louis to sail in search of the Mexican cruiser, the young revenue captain had heard some rumours which led him to suspect that a cargo of wine would be spirited past Manuel's door, from a vessel soon to arrive from Europe. It was with the intention of lying in wait for this vessel that he was about to leave port, and which led him so confidently to write and assure Isabel of his soon seeing her, as the smuggler's cabin was not far distant from her abode. But the orders which he had from the department turned him aside from this object, to pursue one more congenial with his ambition. Nevertheless, inasmuch as he found his schooner becalmed off the entrance of the lake, he determined that while he took that opportunity to pay a visit to Isabel, he would also give the smuggler a call and cast an eye to his movements.

Manuel had very readily admitted his crew of four men into his cabin, being deceived and his fears lulled by the excuse which Louis gave, that he preferred going alone to visit his lady-love, to whom Manuel well knew he was attached. The Spaniard, however, did not intermit his habitual caution, nor dismiss altogether his suspicions of such visitors, whose profession it was to be opposers of his legitimate craft. The men had been drinking wine with him and telling their long yarns, perfectly indifferent themselves, so long as they were not ordered to be vigilant, whether the Spaniard drew their beverage from a cask bearing the excise mark or not. By the time Louis returned a perfect good feeling had been established between the parties, and Manuel felt quite assured that the visit of the revenue officer was what it was represented to be, an affair of love rather than of the laws. This idea was confirmed from the fact that Louis came in a boat with only four men. He, however, was ill at ease, lest some accident might detain them too long; for he had seen that a breeze was springing up, and this event was quite as important a matter to him as it was to Louis, as will be shortly seen.

The young revenue officer having landed and approached the hut from which a light streamed forth, and from which came the voice of a merry song, Manuel threw it open, remarking—

"Your men are very happy, captain!"

"Yes; the dogs know how to enjoy themselves when on shore, and especially when they can pour free wine down their hoarse throats."

"Enter captain. Free, or branded, you are welcome to the best my poor hut affords."

Louis entered the large apartment, in the centre of which stood a table, which from the iron rings upon its feet, had plainly been in the cabin of some vessel. Around this board were seated his four men, two of them with grey heads, and grizzly beards, looking as if they had faced the tempests of a quarter of a century; and the other two, bold, reckless-looking young men, in blue roundabouts, and tarpaulins. Before them stood a large earthen jug of water, which was flanked by several bottles, empty, full, and half-filled with ruby wine. As Louis entered they were in the act of drinking his health; for he was a very popular officer with all who sailed under him.

"Thanks, my lads," he said, in hearty tone; "thanks. The same to you, and a successful cruise for the little Ringdove."

This sentiment, uttered by their captain, just as he was entering the door, was ceived by them with a loud shou which wound up in a regular huzza.

"Don't be noisy, lads. I fear you have taken too much grape juice for ballast. You have a twelve mile pull before you to-night; and too much wine makes woman's nerves."

"We'll drink no more, captain," answered one of the men, rising and touching his hat with an air of tipsy respect for his commander. "The Spanish Don

Smugglaro here keeps the true juice. It is my sworn belief, saving yer presence, captain, that all wine as goes through the custom-house is watered."

"It is not polite, Ben," said one of the young men, "to give out the idea that this never paid duty. If I thought it had never paid duty, it would have gone against my conscience to have drank a drop.

"There, captain," said Manuel, handing to him a bottle and glass, "there is a wine that Mahomet gives to his followers in Paradise. Try it, and say if my brother's vineyard be not a rare one."

"You say well, Manuel," answered Louis, after drinking a full bumper, and setting down the glass; "when I go to Oporto I shall not fail to trespass on his hospitality. Does he not make more than this one cask, which he so fraternally sends you annually?"

"I am not inquisitive, captain," answered the Spaniard, dryly. "I have never asked my brother about his business. I am content to receive his gift, and commend him to the saints for his reward, in remembering a poor fisherman, who but for him would never have known the colour of wine."

"Come, my lads, to the boat again, and be ready to start at a moment's notice!"

The four seamen left the hut, touching their hats as they passed their captain, and got into the boat.

"It is well I returned as I did, Manuel, or you would have got all four of my men fairly drunk with your nectar of Mahomet's paradise," said Louis, seeing that one of his men reeled a little, as he walked down to the boat.

"No, senor," answered Manuel, in a tone of remarkable significence; "I do not care to have tipsy men in my hut, and especially to-night. The sooner I get rid of them the better."

"Why not care to have them particularly to-night?" asked Louis.

"Did I say to-night?" asked Manuel, quickly. "I meant at any time, not to-night more than at any other time. I kept them sober out of respect to you."

"I am much obliged to you, Manuel. But doubtless the severe discipline I keep up over my men helped their sobriety somewhat. But where is your fair daughter, the lovely dark-eyed Benita?"

"She is in the city with her aunt, senor," answered Manuel, abruptly, as if he did not much like to reply or speak of her at all. "The wind is rising away here," he said, raising his arms and turning the palm of his hand towards the south and west. You will have wind enough outside by the time you reach your schooner, capitan."

"Yes, and I shall welcome it when it comes!"

"Your men say you are bound on a cruise off the Tortugas, after a privateer, that has been cruising between there and the Cape Antonio, the last month. This wind that is rising will be fair for a run to the west of Cuba. I wish you success, captain."

"Thank you. Do you know, Manuel, that next to capturing this privateer, I have the greatest desire to catch you running a cargo of wine through the bay up to the city?"

This was spoken in a laughing manner. Manuel changed colour, and for a moment let his dark glance rest upon the face of the young officer, with the most intense suspicion. But he saw nothing to confirm his fears, nothing to lead him to suppose that he had any more reason for making the remark then, than at any other time; for he had heard Louis say the same thing before; and well knew that frankly and freely as he treated him, he would pounce upon him the first time he could catch him infringing the revenue laws.

"Bien, senor, if you find more wine enter the mouth of this creek than my one cask, you are welcome to it."

"I well know, good Manuel, that that one cask should be most correctly rendered with two or perhaps three cyphers added to the figure one. But I shall keep sharp watch!"

"And so shall I, senor captain," answered the Spaniard with a laugh, as he led the way to the boat, with the anxious manner of a host, who wishes to get rid of his guest as soon as may be, and who apprehends evil from his lingering.

Louis stepped into the boat, and as he did so, extended his hand to the smuggler, who, in spite of his being a revenue officer, and the most active one of the coast, liked him though he watched him.

"Good bye, Manuel. Remember me to thy fair daughter. I have seen her but once, and that once has made me think thee the happiest of fathers in having one so beautiful to cheer thee in thy solitary home."

"My daughter is well enough, senor," answered Manuel. "This wind, will aid thee, for I see thou hast a sail in the bottom of thy boat."

"Yes, I took it to help us if a breeze should spring up. Adios, Manuel."

"Adios, senor," answered the old man, waving his hand with a graceful salutation.

"Give way, men," cried Louis, and the boat, turning her prow towards the lake, moved rapidly away from the smuggler's landing, and in a moment or two, passed out of the inlet beneath the overhanging curtain of branches, into the moonlight. Here Louis hoisted the sail, and taking the helm, stretched boldly across the lake, in the direction of its outlet.

CHAPTER IV.

THE BROTHER AND SISTER.

ROBERT ROSAL walked rapidly on towards the villa in advance of Isabel. He was greatly agitated by the discovery he had made. His strongest fears had been confirmed. His sister and his greatest enemy—the man he hated above all men for his name and blood—were lovers! He had found them together, and they had not feared to confess their attachment.

Nor is their love to be wondered at. The residence of Colonel Dumont was less than a league distant from the villa. He had once been Mr. Rosal's most intimate friend. Together they went forth from their estates to offer their services in the cause of their country; and side by side bravely fought on the 8th of January; and more than once had they contributed to each other's safety. After the war they returned to their respective estates, married, and in a few weeks each of them had a son and daughter to take up their attention and to build up bright hopes for the future upon. Daily the fathers saw one another, and loved to speak of the probable two-fold union between their children. They delighted to see them together, and with joy watched their childish attachment.

"Louis will be Isabel's wife one day," said Mr. Rosal with a smile of happiness, as the two fathers were gazing upon the sports of the four children.

"Yes, colonel, and Robert will wed Mary. It will be hands across. We shall be united together, my friend, by double links through this union of our children!"

In this manner did the two fathers discourse of their children. But this serene course of life was not destined long to continue. It was unhappily interrupted by the bitter and contentious spirit of politics. It was a period when party feeling was running high. Families were divided against themselves individually, and a difference of opinion separated brothers. The two gentlemen took opposite sides, and at length when they met, their conversation took a political turn. The chances of their favorite candidates were at first calmly discussed; but as each warmed with his subject he seemed to think himself only in the right, and the other wrong. Conviction of being on the right side, led to a desire on the part of each to convince the other of error. This attempt at conversion led to warm words, and ultimately to an open quarrel. It was as sudden as it was violent, and epithets of the most insulting character passed between those who but a few moments before were the firmest friends. The rupture became so wide, and the spirit of acrimony so strong in each breast, that for several weeks the friendly intercourse between them entirely ceased. Mutual friends at length succeeded in reconciling them; but in a few days the subject was once more started, and from bitter words they came to blows. Mr. Rosal, with angry violence slapped Colonel Dumont in the face, at the same time applying to him the terms of "idiot," and "fool."

But for the intervention of friends the degraded officer would have wiped out the stain upon his honour with the blood of his insulter. He was compelled to keep his sword in its sheath, from which it had half leaped to avenge the gross injury he had received at the hand of his former friend.

A challenge followed, and the parties met. Mr. Rosal being the challenged party, regulated the conditions of the combat, to which, with reluctance, Colonel Dumont consented. They were, that they should fight with swords, and that the combat should continue until one of the parties fell dead or cried for quarter.

The result of the contest is already known to the reader. Colonel Dumont, after having received his antagonist's sword five times in his arm and body, brought him to his knees, and called upon him to yield. But Mr. Rosal replied only by making an upward lunge at his heart, when the sword of Dumont passed to the hilt into his breast. Mr. Rosal fell over upon his side and died without a word or a struggle.

The victor stood gazing upon him with looks of the deepest grief All his former friendship for him now rushed back upon his soul. Tears came to his eyes, and kneeling by his side he took his lifeless hand and bathed it with the moisture of profound sorrow.

His friends came to him and warned him to fly. He embraced the body of his friend, and mounting a horse, galloped away, accompanied by one or two of his friends. On his way he stopped a few moments at his house, commended his children to the care of his weeping wife, and in an hour afterwards was on board a vessel on his way to Cuba.

The versions of this painful rencontre were two-fold. One party, the friends of Rosal, declared that the conduct of Colonel Dumont had been that of an assassin; that he took the life of his antagonist when it would have been a point of honour to spare it. The other party pronounced the combat to have been strictly in accordance with the rules which were to regulate it, and which were drawn up by the deceased himself; and that unless Colonel Dumont had slain his antagonist he would have fallen a victim to the other's evident and most vindictive determination to kill him.

The latter narrative of the affair had been early impressed upon the minds of Robert and Isabel, who at the death of their father were five and nine years of age. Louis and his sister received the account which defended their father. Louis was eight years of age, and his sister Mary but five, when their father exiled himself to Cuba, to escape the retribution of the laws; for the friends of Mr. Rosal resolved to prosecute him for what they termed his foul murder.

After the absence of two years, and when the affair was blown over, Colonel Dumont secretly returned to his estate. Upon the day of his arrival, his youngest daughter had been lost upon the lake, and he found his wife and Louis in the deepest affliction. It appeared that a negro slave was fishing not far from the shore, when Louis called to him to take them in and row them about. He obeyed, and, by their direction, pulled under some trees which overhung the water, as Louis said he wished to swing by the branches. The slave, fearing to disobey his young master, paddled the canoe under the branches of a large water-oak whose giant limbs extended far out from the bank, and in the dark shade of which the water was black as ink. Here the boat stopped, and Louis catching by the pendant branch of one of the limbs began to swing to and fro, pushing himself far out from the boat, so that he hung over the water. The old negro, seeing that the current was strong there, for the tide was coming in and flowed swiftly up a bayou a few feet distant, endeavoured to prevail upon the adventurous boy to give up his dangerous sport.

"If you break dat limb, massa Louis, you for sartin go plump in de water and be drown dead as 'em fish."

"Never mind me, Cuffo," answered Louis, laughing; "I can swim if the branch should break."

As he spoke he pushed against the side of the boat with his foot, to give himself a wider swing, and with such sudden force as to throw his sister, who was clapping her hands, and watching with delight his sport, head first over the gunwale into the dark water. The negro uttered a shout of horror, and, unable to swim, seized the oar to attempt her rescue. Louis no sooner saw her disappear than with a shriek he quickly dropped from the limb and dived after her. As he came to the surface without her the blade of Cuffo's oar struck him upon the head with such force as to stun him. The negro grasped him by the hair and drew him into the boat insensible. He then looked around, overcome with terror, in search of the child; but he could no where behold her. She had either sunk at once without rising again, or else risen and drifted away from his sight, underneath the low branches of the trees. Filling the air with lamentations he pulled all around the spot, but in vain. He then turned his attention to Louis, whom he soon revived. The boy's first exclamation was for his sister; and when he was told that she had not come to the surface again he would have plunged in after her, but for the strong grasp which the old slave held upon him.

The intelligence of the loss of the child had hardly been conveyed to Madame Dumont ere her husband suddenly made his appearance. It was a sad hour of arrival; and instead of the smiles of joy which he had been so long anticipating, he was met with the tears of the bereaved mother.

His presence at home was not noticed by his former enemies, who had suffered their hostility to die out with time and reflection. But, although his appearance abroad was unattended with danger he preferred the retirement of his home. The death of his child, to whom he was fondly attached, preyed heavily upon his spirits, and the quiet of his estate was most congenial to the sadness of his heart.

He constantly mourned the fall of his friend by his hand, and bitterly regretted the circumstances which had led to an event so painful. He now devoted himself to the education of his son, who promised to be an honour to his declining years. But Colonel Dumont did not live to see his hopes in his boy matured. His health, impaired by his residence at Cuba, and undermined by his sorrows, at length gave way, and when Louis was in his sixteenth year he died, leaving him the heir of a small patrimony. Previous to his death he had exerted his influence to get his son into the navy, but finding that he could not succeed, he obtained a promise of his admittance into the revenue service, from which he hoped that he would one day make his way into the naval service of his country.

Louis entered the service of the revenue, and was in a very little time promoted to a lieutenancy. He occasionally revisited his native land, where his heart ever lingered, but not so much with his mother, whom he, nevertheless, most tenderly loved, as with Isabel Rosal, the playmate of his childhood, and the partner of many a stolen walk of his riper youth.

The death of Mr. Rosal, which had cast such a cloud over the two families, had not eradicated from the bosom of the beautiful Isabel her childish love for the handsome young Louis. They secretly met, and condoled with each other in tears, over the great misfortune that had come upon them. Louis gave her to understand the truth, exonerating his father; and while both mourned the fatal event, they promised with all the ardour of children that it should never make any difference in their affection for one another.

Faithfully did they adhere to their resolution. Robert, whose more fiery spirit could not brook any intercourse with the son of the man who had taken the life of his father, seeing this intimacy continue, so fearfully menaced his sister, that trembling for her life, she promised he should never see her speak to him again. But she meant, nevertheless, to speak to him as often as she could, unseen by her brother.

In this manner the young people grew up to manhood and womanhood; Louis devoted himself so assiduously to his profession, that he at length rose to command one of the fleetest cutters in the gulf; while Robert, entering the navy, was about the same time promoted to a lieutenancy. The young gentlemen seldom met, but when they did, it was to bow with cold formality.

The vessel of war to which Robert was attached had been ordered, a few weeks prior to the opening of our story, to blockade the Rio Grande. It was there he received intelligence, in a most mysterious way, that if he would save his sister from marrying the son of his father's murderer, he must hasten homeward without delay.

His sudden appearance, and discovery of Louis and Isabel on the cliff we have already witnessed. We now return to him as he was walking back to the villa, greatly agitated at the discovery of his sister's attachment. Slowly Isabel walked on behind him, not wishing, by her presence, to provoke him farther, or endanger her life by coming near him in his present excited state of mind.

Suddenly he stopped, and looking back, called her to hasten her steps.

"Tell me, and tell me truthfully, Isabel, are you betrothed to this assassin's son?"

"I do not recognise any person so designated. If you get an answer from me, Robert, you must use more moderate language."

Robert knew too well the firm and independent spirit of his sister to attempt to browbeat her. He knew that mildness only was the sceptre to which she would in the least bend.

"Are you engaged to Louis Dumont?" he said, in an altered tone.

"Yes."

"And the time set for your marriage, I dare say."

"Yes."

"Pray may I know when it is?" he asked, in the same ironical tone in which he had spoken the last two or three sentences.

"It will be on his return from his present cruise."

"I think I heard him say he was about to go in chase of a Mexican privateer, lately seen cruising off the Tortugas."

"Yes, brother."

"Very well. It is all I wish to know," he answered, entering the house.

CHAPTER V.

THE SMUGGLER'S DAUGHTER.

As Robert Rosal entered the hall he ordered his servant to bring a fresh horse to the door; and after taking some refreshment he went out, and, without saying a word to Isabel, mounted and galloped away alone.

"If it were not that Louis is on the lake in safety within his boat, I should fear he would get some mischief from my brother," she said, as she saw him ride furiously away. "Did your master say which way he was going, or whether he should return to-night?" she inquired of the black groom.

"No, missis. He nebber say noting. He look berry angry and swear at him horse and use him spur mighty hard. I reckons mass' Robert berry sick or some'at else is ails him! Dat's my sartain 'piniun, missis!"

"Very well, Jemmy. You can go to your room."

"Tankey, missis! It be midnight if be anyting at all. Dare's de tin dipper ober de long chimney, wid de handle pointin' up de sky."

With this astronomical observation, the old negro shuffled along through the wide open hall towards the court-yard in the rear; while Isabel, full of anxiety, and restless from the events of the night, unable to seek repose, resolved once more to retrace her steps to the cliff and watch if, perchance, she might discover her lover's retiring boat, and thus be assured of his safety; for that Robert's departure boded injury to Louis she had not the remotest doubt. His manner and his last words to her confirmed this suspicion.

Finding that the house was all quiet again, she stole forth and hurried to the cliff. It was now half an hour past midnight. The full moon had passed the zenith, and was beginning to descend the western arch of the sky. There was a coolness in the air that is peculiar to the midnight hour, and a stillness that made the heart instinctively suppress its throbbings.

She walked quickly on, and soon reached the low wooded headland where her brother had discovered her with Louis. The moonlit lake was spread out before her, sparkling in the beams of light, as the rising breeze dimpled its placid bosom. The same breeze lifted the dark tresses from her brow and neck, and rustled amid the foliage of the trees above her head.

"He had a sail in his boat. This welcome breeze will bear him quickly to his vessel and away from danger. My brother in his anger is capable of anything; and the suspicion presses upon my mind that he has galloped to some of the fishermen's huts to get a boat and assistance to intercept him. But with this wind Louis will escape his enemies. Though it will bear him farther and farther from me each instant, yet I rejoice in seeing it strengthen its force. Perhaps if I look closely across the water I may discover his white sail, the signal to me of his safety."

She bent her eyes over the water and looked long and earnestly, but could see nothing save the silvered sheen of the waves flashing in the moonbeams as far as her vision could penetrate into the shining haze that hurried over the horizon. She was about turning away with disappointment and apprehension lest he should have returned as he came around the bend of the lake, and so be exposed to any boat from the shore, when with a joyful exclamation she extended both hands in a direction to the right towards the western shore of the lake. A snowy sail was visible less than a league off and standing eastward.

"He is safe! It is Louis and he is safe from my brother!" was her glad cry. "He has hoisted his sail and will ere long be on the deck of his vessel. My joy at his escape from my brother's vengence leads me almost to forget the peril in which he is about to be placed. But I commit him to the care of Him who has hitherto watched over us. Perhaps in two weeks he may return a conqueror, and then my happiness will be complete, for he will return to claim me as his bride. Oh! happy bride! oh! sweet bridal! when two hearts that have so long and faithfully loved shall be one never to be dissevered!"

Filled with these pleasant thoughts, she seated herself upon a gnarled root of the old oak that grew above her, and watched with love's untiring eye the distant sail of her lover's boat. She knew it was his. The instinct of love told her that beneath its silvery shield sat the form dearer than all else to her on earth. She sat watching the little sail till it faded in the distance across the lake, till the memory of its image alone remained upon the retina of her eye.

"Farewell, noble Louis!" she sighed, "If the prayers of a true and fond heart will avail, thou wilt soon return with honour. But what do I see! There is another boat; it is a lugger with two sails, just creeping out from the land, with oars as numerous as the feet of a centipede. With oars and sails she gathers headway and is in hot pursuit. It must be Robert, who has, by the aid of gold, got the assistance of fishermen to go out and try to overtake Louis ere he reaches his vessel. Heaven protect him and send him safe beyond the reach of his foes. Would that the wind would now die away! There are full ten oars by the movements, and they move rapidly.—Louis is already more than half way to his schooner, and if he does not loiter will reach it in safety. Oh! that I had wings to fly and inform him of the enemy that is pursuing him, and urge him to fly with oar and sail."

MANUEL ASSISTING HIS DAUGHTER ON SHORE.

She rose up and watched with the most eager anxiety the progress of this new object upon the hitherto quiet lake. It was in truth a large lugger, such as was used by fishermen in the Gulf. It carried two low sails, which shone brightly in the moonlight, and appeared to be urged on its way by eight or ten oars. It moved, however, slowly, compared with the light and swift motion of the boat which had gone before it and was full two leagues ahead.

Isabel watched it until she saw it, like the one of which it was doubtless in chace,

No. 3

fade away in the distant white haze that hung upon the horizon.   She then began to dwell most painfully upon the dangers of her lover ; and amid tears and prayers for his safety, she sank weariedly into deep sleep.

Leaving her to her happy, oblivious repose, with the moonlight shining upon her darkly lashed eyes and alabaster brow, and turning into diamonds the tears upon her cheeks, with her head resting like a child's upon one arm, and the breeze from the lake fanning her veined temples, we will return to the hut of Manuel, the fisherman.

The cutter's boat, in which Louis had left the creek, had no sooner passed out of sight beneath the overhanging branches that shut in its mouth, than Manuel ooked like a man greatly relieved.   He breathed heavily and breathed freely two or three times, and then said aloud—

"Thank the saints and the blessed Virgin, he is gone and his men with him. I feared that they really suspected my business to-night, and meant to stay my guests, whether invited or no, till morning.   Well, I am safely rid of this sharp young captain ; and I hope I shall not see his face again until I get my cargo ashore and fairly smuggled through.   It is a rare escape ; and I may thank my stars that a Mexican privateer has befriended me to-night.   There goes his boat, the sail up, and running straight across the lake," he added, moving a little way along the bank by his hut, where an opening in the trees gave him a vista of the bright waters beyond.

He then turned to enter his cabin, when his quick ear caught the dip of an oar in the water up the creek.   He stopped and listened, for he could see nothing, the trees overarched the bay so closely, forming a sort of umbrageous tunnel beneath.

" It is 'Nita.   I know the stroke of her paddle in a hundred.   She has returned soon !"

He descended to the side of the water, and leaped into one of the luggers boats, which was drawn up on the land, and looking up the narrow but deep creek, by stooping so as to see beneath the folliage, he distinctly beheld a boat gliding down towards him.   An opening in the branches above it, let in the moonlight for an instant, and fell upon the face and form of a young girl, who was standing in the stern of a small light pirogue, and skilfully and rapidly paddling it down the stream.

The next moment she gracefully brought the skiff along side of the boat in which the smuggler stood, and sprang into it.

"You are returned in good time, 'Nita," he said, taking her hand, and then kissing with prideful affection her brown but handsome cheek.

" I was not delayed in town," she responded, in a richly-keyed voice, the accents of which were perfectly musical,—"I found Monsieur Delforme at his house, and gave him the information you sent by me !"

" Prompt and faithful, 'Nita, like yourself," said the smuggler, laying his hand kindly upon her brow.   " You would have been an hero, had you been a man.   It is in you anyhow.   What said Monsieur Delforme ?"

" He told me to tell you that your readiness should not go unrewarded ; and that everything should be prepared as heretofore for receiving the freight you forward."

" Bueno !   That is all I want.   Now come in and take some coffee, and then go to bed ; for you must be tired with this long paddle of three leagues and more."

" No, father.   The current helped me for the first two leagues ; and the moon shone so brightly that the labour was rather a pleasure than a toil.   But who has been with you, sir ?" she asked quickly, as she entered the cabin and saw the signs of the recent visit of the cutter's crew.

" Some of my old friends from the Ringdove," he answered, laughing. —" They staid but an hour, and have just gone."

" From the Ringdove—Who ?   Was he among them?"

" Whom do you mean ?" asked the smuggler, staring.

"I mean was Captain Louis among them?"

"Faith he was, and went with them too. If you will take two steps aside from the door and bend your glance between the trees you will see his white sail, on his return to his vessel."

"Just gone. Would that I had been here sooner !" she said with a deep emotion. "Did he ask for me?"

" That he did, I'll be bound. You never see one of these young officers forget a bright eye when they had once seen it."

"What did he ask?" inquired the young girl, who seemed wholly indifferent to everything but the visit of the young captain of the cutter. "I would have given my eyes to have seen him.'

"No, no. Your eyes are worth a pair of royal diamonds each. You can see him for less price, girl, by-and-bye ; for he will be cruising here again in a month or so ; after I have cleverly got my casks of wine to the city. Come, drink this coffee. It is the best cup I have ever made, I'm thinking."

"No, father. I can talk only of this young sailor."

" Then more's the folly that you can't. He cares little for you, girl, though he did ask for you. Besides, what would he have to say to a poor fisherman's daughter but that she should blush to hear named. You have seen him once, and that is enough. Nay, if this is the way the wind blows, it is once too much. He has a lady in his eye and in his heart too, I am thinking.'

" I know it, sir," she answered with all the nervous quickness of jealous love. "But he will never wed her."

" Nor will he ever wed thee. So put him out of thy mind, and drink thy coffee and go to bed. If this wind blows up sharply it may bring the Portuguese brig in to-night. We shall then have enough to do. I will go and take a look out eastward, and see if anything is moving."

With these words the old man reached up to a pair of beckets, placed over the rude pallet which formed his couch, and taking from them a spy-glass, covered with old and well greased canvass, went out and mounted a flight of rude stairs that led from the ground at the western end of his hut to its roof. He ascended to a sort of platform, which was built around the chimney, and from which he had an uninterrupted prospect of the lake in the direction of the outlet. Placing his glass to his eye, he began to sweep the offing with great closeness and attention.

The young girl remained in the hut. She seated herself at the table and placing her cheek in her hand (it was very small hand, soft and exquisitely shaped, though as brown as berry) and seemed to be brooding over sad thoughts. The light of the smuggler's iron lamp fell softly upon her, and revealed a very handsome face. Dark brown hair, soft and flowing, dark Arabian eyes, and the most bewitching rosy ripe mouth that ever was moulded by Cupid for a lover's temptation. She was slight and small in figure, but as graceful as an antelope. She wore a green silk handkerchief, bound with a a charming effect about her brow, its colour contrasting finely with the hazel, sun-browned hue of her pretty forehead. The brows were arches, and as black as if drawn accurately with charcoal. The eyes that burned beneath were full of fire and expression—the expression of womanly feeling rather than of mind. Yet her face was intelligent, and strongly marked with good sense, and self-confidence which gives point to character. Her form, though she could not have been more than seventeen or eighteen, was the perfection of womanhood in the soft undulation of its modest, yet voluptuous outline. She was a little Hebe, and made to be loved and to love. Well might old Manuel be proud of her.

CHAPTER VI.

THE LOOK-OUT.

THE meditations of the young girl were suddenly interrupted by the sound of her father's voice, calling to her from his look-out on the roof.

"Ho, 'Nita, come up hither."

"What is it, sir?" she asked, rising and going to the door.

"Your eyes are younger and sharper than mine. I want you to see what you make out of what I have caught sight of."

The young girl lightly mounted to the roof by the steep stair-way and after glancing over the bright waters, said—

"What is it you see, sir?"

"It looks to me like a sail in the offing. But take the glass and see what you can make of it with your bright eyes," said Manuel, slowly removing the old spy-glass from his right eye and placing it in her hands. "Not that way, girl. You are looking at the cutter's boat. Turn the glass four points further east."

"I will in a moment, father," answered Benita, who had caught sight of the boat in which Louis was making the best of his way to rejoin his vessel; and she continued to watch it as if she had been called up to the roof for no other purpose. The old smuggler grew impatient, and taking the glass by the extremity, he turned it round and levelled it in the direction of the opening to the gulf.

"That is the direction girl," he said, almost sternly, though rarely did he ever speak sharply to her. "Now, what do you make of her!"

"There is a vessel, sir, plainly."

"So I could have sworn, though I was not quite sure till your eyes had seen her too. What is she? Can you tell that too?"

"Two masts, father. But whether a schooner, or brig, I cannot tell."

"You have told enough. All I wanted to know was, whether it was a vessel at all. It is as faint as a wreath of mist on the lake in the break of morning."

"I make out, distinctly, that it is a vessel, sir, though very far off."

"Yes. Full twelve miles, if one. It may be the Ring Dove, which I know is off there, but I rather suspect it is our brig; for she looks square-rigged, as well as I can make her out. How does she seem to you?"

"Going away very fast, father. She will soon disappear. Oh, that I could have seen him once more. The sail is now diminished to a point."

"What are you talking about, girl?" cried Manuel; and looking, he saw that the glass was no longer directed towards the offing and the strange sail, but turned upon Louis's little boat, which seemed alone to occupy her thoughts. "The child is bewitched. Give me the glass, 'Nita, and go to bed. I am glad for your sake that you did not see this young officer to-night. He seems to have got into your head like a glass of wine. Stay, before you go down, answer me soberly, and truly, one or two questions."

This was spoken with an impressive voice, and he laid his hand, as he addressed her, firmly, but kindly, upon her shoulder, while his eyes from beneath their thick, grey brows, gazed closely in upon her own dark orbs.

"Say what you please, father, I will listen," she answered, dropping her eyes beneath his scorching gaze, and looking as if she anticipated the inquiries he was about to make of her.

"Have you seen this captain of the Ringdove more than once? Have you seen him since the time, three months ago, he staid half the day in my house here, till the storm which detained him, passed over? Then I know you talked with him, and seemed to take pleasure in his society; and truly, he is a young gentle-man well fitted to please a maiden's eye; but it should be a maiden of his own rank and order, not one so lowly as thou art. Thy virtue and good name

Smuggler's daughter, as men call thee, are all that thou hast. They should be cherished as the apple of the eye. Hast thou seen him since that time, that thou goest nigh wild when thou art told he has been here, and gone, unseen by thee? Answer me truly, child. For I ask for thy good. Thy happiness is dearer to me than my own life. Thou hast been an angel in my lonely home, to bless it, and I should be an ingrate not to try to make thee happy. Freely and frankly, answer me!"

"I have seen him since, dear father!" she answered firmly, though with deep blushes, heightening the rich brown beauty of her cheeks.

"I supected as much. I could not believe that such deep, nervous interest as you have shown in him to-night, could have got head out of that one interview, and I present nearly the whole of the three hours that he was in the hut. When and where was it thou didst meet him?"

"Eight weeks ago, father. It was by accident. It was when you sent me to the city, to aunt Josefina, to stay a week. I was at vespers in the Cathedral, kneeling, and devoutly engaged in my prayers, and telling my beads—the string of costly pearl beads which you gave me my last birth-day. I was not looking about me. I was thinking only of my prayers, and did not know any young gentleman was regarding me. Somehow, as I was running my beads over, the string which held them parted, and my pearls fell to the pavement, and went rolling away from me on all sides. I sprung to feet my to recover them, and was assisted by two or three female slaves that were kneeling near me, and soon had them all but one, the largest of them all. While I was looking round to discover this, a young gentleman came up and bowing held it out to me, saying that he had found it under the railing of the chancel. As I looked up to thank him, I recognised—"

"Louis Dumont, I'll be sworn, for a peso!" interrupted Manuel, with a smile, though his words were abruptly uttered.

"Yes, sir. He also recognised me and exclaimed—'Dona Benita! Is it my happiness once more to have the good fortune to see you, and to do this slight service for you?'"

"A very pretty speech doubtless. And what reply made the Dona Benita?"

"I thanked him, sir, for the pearl, and without making any reply, I bowed and left the Cathedral."

"And did he leave too?"

"He did, sir."

"So I guessed; and followed thee?"

"I could not help it, sir."

"And spoke to thee, too?"

"Yes, sir."

"And you could not help answering?"

"No, sir."

"He accompanied thee to thy aunt Josefina's, I'll wager thee?"

"The street was his to walk in, sir. I could not prevent his walking whither he would."

"Even by thy side if he chose?"

"No, sir."

"And made he love to thee, girl?" demanded the old Spaniard something sharply.

"No, father."

"I dare say he only talked to thee of the Saints and Heaven, and thou didst answer him in kind. He went to the step o' the door with thee, did he?"

"Yes, father."

"Did he go in?"

"No, sir. Nor have I seen him since."

"So then he parted from thee there. Was it with a kiss?"

"It was broad sun-light, sir."

"Then had there been moonlight for the sunlight, he would have kissed thee?'

"I do not know, sir. He but took my hand as he left, and bidding me good bye, said he should not soon forget me."

"And I dare swear you said as much to him?"

"I know, father, the modesty becoming a maiden, wild and rude as has been the way in which I have been brought up. I said not that I should never forget him; but I felt in my heart that I never should."

"This then, is all."

"Save that I remember him daily, and am happiest when thinking of him.— This pearl will always bring him to my thoughts."

As she spoke, she raised a large central pearl of a row that hung about her neck to her lips, and touched it with love's simple, but ardent devotion. Old Manuel shook his head. The frank, artless, undisguised statement made by his daughter had caused him painful feelings. He saw at once that the young sailor had won, perhaps unknowingly, her young warm heart; and that unless the passion, yet in its infancy, was checked in its growth, it would destroy her peace. He was deeply attached to the lovely girl. Rude as his life was, he had brought her up with the tenderness of a cherished house plant. He had taught her all he knew, and what was beyond his knowledge was communicated by his sister in the city, an old Spanish woman, poor but pious, who initiated her into the mysteries of needle-work, and other feminine handicraft. But the most of her time was passed in the cabin of old Manuel, whom she assisted in his fishing, and as she grew older, aided materially in his smuggling operations. The young girl, ignorant of the nice distinctions in national law, saw no crime in evading the excise duties. If she ever had a question of the lawfulness of smuggling arise in her mind, old Manuel had smugglers' logic to meet it, and overthrow every scruple.

With natural independence of character, and a certain wild freedom of conduct, the necessary result of her mode of life in such a home as Manuel's, she retained that sense of maidenly propriety and innate modesty which will always command the respect of the modest. Not a breath had ever tainted her good name, among those of her own class, though she was often thrown into the companionship of the young fishermen of the lake as she accompanied her father in his pursuits.

Manuel had listened to her confession of love for Louis with painful interest. He was sorrowful that she should place her affections, not only upon one who was her superior, but upon one who could not return them were he her equal. While he felt pity for his daughter, indignation towards Louis kindled in his breast. He well knew that he was betrothed to Isabel Rosal, and that his business up the lake this very night was to visit her, to say farewell before he departed on his cruise. He accused the young seaman of treachery and duplicity.

"Benita," he said, gravely, and looking deeply troubled, "the past may not be recalled, but the future is in our hands, and we may do with it what we choose. This young man is not only above you in rank, but he has no heart to you in return for the noble gift of your own. He did wrong to say that he would never forget you. Those words inspired in you hopes that can never be realised. Louis Dumont is betrothed to Isabel Rosal!"

"I know it, father," she answered, firmly.

"Then why do you love him?" he exclaimed, with a look of surprise.

"I cannot but love him. Besides, sir, I know he will never marry her?"

"You know it? How can you prevent it' Rumour hath it they will soon be wedded. How know you this that you speak so positively?'

"I believe that they will never marry," she responded with hesitation, and such confusion that he regarded her with amazement; for hitherto he had seen only openness and candour in all that she did and said.

"You shall learn, dear father. I fear that you may be angry with me. But I cannot controul the impulse to which my love urges me. The first moment I beheld Louis Dumont enter the door of the cabin, three months ago, I loved him. He spoke, and my heart hung upon his words. He smiled, and my soul was lighted up with joy. It was a happy three hours. I could have prayed that the storm might have thundered over our heads for ever, so that I could bask within the sunshine of his presence!"

"Was it so, girl? I ne'er suspected it!" said Manuel, partly surprised and partly in sympathy; for at bottom the old smuggler had a generous and kind heart, and dearly loved the beautiful girl to whom he was, as it were, now acting the stern part of father confessor.

"It was so, father. When he departed he took my heart with him."

"This is amazing! And did he seek to win your heart!" asked Manuel, angrily.

"Oh, no, father! It seemed to me he loved more to talk with you than with me. But as I looked and listened at his words I loved!"

"This is strange. I saw nothing —must have been blind. Forget him, child! —He cares not for you. He did wrong to speak to you at vespers!"

"He could not return me the pearl, sir, without speaking."

"True. I had forgot that! But he, loving another, should not have walked by thy side. But perhaps he did not know the mischief he was doing. But it was wrong altogether for him to say he would never forget thee."

"It made no difference to me, father. I should never have forgotten him!"

"You are in a bad state, Benita! I would to the saints you had never met."

"Mischief, I fear, will come of this. The best he can do is to marry Mademoiselle Rosal as soon as possible. This will cure you, and save much evil work in the end."

"He can never marry Isabel Rosal, father," answered Benita with extraordinary energy.

"Ho! What is this? Why so? Will you kill him, hey? This comes to a pass by San Diego? Can't marry her?"

But Benita made not reply. She took advantage of her father's surprise and vehement words to escape down the stairs and re-enter the hut.

CHAPTER VII.

THE HORSEMAN.

"CAN'T marry Isabel Rosal?" repeated Manuel several times as he once more placed his spy-glass to his eye. "What does the girl mean. She put an emphasis on her words that meant something; I am sorry for the child. Louis Dumont has done her great injury by showing her attention. But perhaps he did not know the impression he had made upon her heart. For his sake I trust not. But he should have been truer to Isabel Rossal than to have said to 'Nita he should never forget her. These words would show that he thought of her more than he ought. When next I see the youth I will talk with him. Benita must not be trifled with, and this mischievous love between them must be stopped where it is. Evil will come on't else!"

Manuel had now brought the glass to his eye and once more levelled it in the direction of the vessel which he had before discerned, and which could not yet be seen with the naked eye. He could not now see her at all. After looking for her for some time he turned the glass upon the little boat which contained the captain of the Ringdove, and which was still visible with the glass, though at a great distance off.

"The captain makes good way," muttered the old man. "He will soon be aboard his craft, and the sooner the better. I would like well to know what sail that was and what it was about there in the offing; for sail it was, and a brig at least ; though possibly it might have been the cutters' schooner after all, laying by for her captain !   But, it is more likely to be the Portuguese !"

The vessel, which he thus designated, was one of the regular traders between Portugal and New Orleans.   She had been seven years making two voyages annually between Europe and Lake Borgne, freighted principally with choice wines. Her consignees were merchants in New Orleans, Delforme & Co., and Manuel was the chief agent in unloading her cargoes and putting them through to the city by the inland passage of the bayou which had an outlet within a few miles of the port.   This bayou was navigable for batteaux only, and only for these at flood tide. It wound its tortuous way through the level and dense forests of the lake region, in the rear of the plantations.   It had been for many years the haunt of smugglers and even of buccaniers, who had kept possession of it in the very face of the laws, and successfully opposed or evaded every force that had been sent to dislodge them. At length they were broken up by the war, and for some years the smuggling ceased, and the bayou was supposed to have been choked up by the drains of alluvian from the adjacent land.   Manuel the fisherman, however, who had been long a resident of the lake shore, knew well that it was open, and navigable at high tide.   But he kept the secret to himself, and by means of it he was able always to be the earliest in the New Orleans market with gulf fish.   At length, it chanced that a vessel from Lisbon laden mostly with wines, bound to New Orleans, was driven into the lake and wrecked not far from Manuel's usual fishing ground.   He obtained about a score of casks of wine, and secretly conveyed them by the bayou to the city and sold them, free of duty, to Delforme & Co, for a round price. This led to an understanding between them; for this house had the reputatation of having been once engaged in smuggling with Lafitte by the way of the Barritaria bay, and Manuel well knew with whom he had to do.

It was arranged between them that he should be as their accomplice or agent at Lake Borgne, and there receive and secretly convey by batteaux to the city such casks of wine, silk goods, and other articles, as might be brought into the lake by a vessel selected for the purpose.

Under this arrangement Manuel had in the past seven years been the successful instrument in transporting through the bayou no less than eleven cargoes of wine and other freight.   The vessels usually arrived twice in a year, and as near the same day as possible.   That information might be seasonably conveyed to Manuel, he was in league with Pierre, a fisherman who dwelt on one of the Chandeleur isles, and who at the time the vessel was expected to arrive was actively on the look out. Upon her arrival off the islands, Pierre would hoist the sail of his little pirogue and sail up the lake to convey the intelligence to Manuel, who in like manner, would despatch Benita to his employers.   Thus by the time the brig could manage to steal into the lake under cover of the night, all parties would be ready for her reception, and at hand to dispose of her cargo.   Rumours of Manuel's agency in such a contraband business had been of late unusually active; and Louis resolved that the strictest watch should be kept on the old Spaniard, so that if possible he might entrap him.   For this purpose he often paid him a visit, in a friendly way, to talk over the news of the day, and at the same time act as a spy.   He could, however discover nothing to confirm the rumours.   Manuel suspected the true object of the captain's visit, and while he received him hospitably he was cautiously on his guard ; and Louis left him without having made any other discovery than that the beauty of the old smuggler's daughter fully bore out the praises he had heard of it.

The young captain was about preparing for a second visit, when, as we have seen, he received orders to cruise in the Gulf after the Mexican.   Although these orders were received by him with joy, yet he was not a little disappointed that the opportunity to pounce upon Manuel was thus lost; for through his spies and inquiries he had not only satisfied himself that a vessel unloaded opposite Manuel's door once or twice every year, but at the same season every year, and that season was now at hand.   It was, therefore, quite as much with an eye to take a peep into the bay and drop in upon Manuel, as to have an interview with Isabel, that he left his schooner and pulled up the lake.

He was not far out in his information.   That very afternoon Pierre's little skiff had landed at Manuel's and brought to him the intelligence that the expected brig was lying nine miles off the Chandeleur Isles, and if the wind served would make her run up that night.   This information was communicated by Manuel to Benita, and jumping into the pirogue, the fearless girl bore it to the city.   On her return, when within about a mile of the Lake, she passed a hut hidden among the trees, to

BETINA, BY HER HEROIC CONDUCT SAVES THE LIFE OF ROBERT ROSA.

a stake near which was tied a league square batteaux.   She stopped paddling as she came near it, slightly grazd it in passing, and taking from beneath the seat upon which she sat a small sharp arrow, to which was attached a little red flag, she stuck it into the stern of the batteau, and then, with a horn that hung at her girdle, she wound three shrill blasts and darted again on her way.   Half a mile further down she passed another circular hut and batteau fastened near it, into which she threw an arrow and a second time wound her horn.   Before the echoes in the first case had died away in the silence of the dark forest, the door of the hut opened and

No. 4.

a man came forth, and blew a horn loudly in response; and then calling up two others, who slept within, the three proceeded to unmoor the batteau and embark in her towards the lake.—At the second hut the occupants, two tall men, were slower in making their appearance; but they responded with a blast from a horn as the former had done, and also prepared to embark. In less than half an hour both batteaux were slowly floating down the sluggish current of the bayou, now seen as they passed an open space in the forest, where moonlight could make its way, now invisible in the darkness of the overhanging branches that arched the stream, and which compelled them most of the time to stoop to avoid contact with them.

Manuel remained upon the roof of his cabin, with his glass at his eye for some minutes after Benita descended, but he could see nothing more of the vessel; and believing that both had been deceived by their wishes, he glanced an instant at the little white speck, all that appeared of the boat in which Louis was flying towards the gulf, and was preparing to go down again, when the sound of horses' feet along the sands of the lake shore arrested his ear.

"Who can that be?" he exclaimed, listening and endeavouring to penetrate the thick trees which interposed between himself and the beach. There was a horseman's road at low and half-tides along the borders of the lake; but it was rarely travelled, especially at that hour of the night. "Benita," he called to the maiden, who was walking up and down in front of the door, with a firm, spirited step and an air of troubled thought; for she was dwelling upon the madness and folly of her passion for the young seamen, yet still feeling that rather than forget him she would rather love in despair.

"But I will not despair," she cried vehemently; "he may yet forget Isabel Rosal for the bar is already placed to his union with her. Then, when he is cast off there, he will remember me. He has told me, oh! sweet words, that he would never forget me. How dear is this reflection to my soul. I will love, though to love were to perish. Oh, that he knew how my heart worshipped him! But, but——"

"Benita, ho!"

"Sir," she answered, recalled to herself after being hailed for the third time by her father.

"One might as well have no ears as not to hear with them."

"Sir. What is it?"

"Do you not hear that horse galloping."

"Yes, sir."

"Go to the lake shore and see who it is. It is all but a chance it may be some one coming to see me. Yet, they may ride by, up to the black-boy settlements."

Benita heard the echoing hoofs as they fell upon the hard sand of the lake shore. she at once hastened to obey her father, and with unusual alacrity, for her curiosity was excited by the rare event of a horseman scouring along the beach at night though by day, occasionally a negro slave in search of stray cattle, or an overseer pursuing a run-away, would pass along the lake shore.

We have said that the cabin of Manuel was situated a few rods in the rear of the lake and on the bank of a narrow dark creek that made up from it; that not only the hut was invisible to one sailing by on the lake, but the entrance to the inlet itself could be discovered only by one familiar with it, or who watched the current flowing outward. A shady path led from Manuel's house straight to the lake. This path was now taken by Benita, and she soon stood where she could command the beach for some distance. As the trees stretched far over the beach and dipped into the water, the road which she surveyed was, save here and there where a moon beam crossed it, intensely dark. Yet, in motion, through the alternate light and shade, she distinctly saw a horseman advancing. As he came to the creek he plunged boldly in and in a few seconds landed on the side where she stood, and within twenty feet of her. Without stopping, he spurred up the bank with a bold familiarity of one who had before been the same path, and gaining the place where she stood, was about galloping towards the hut, when, at the sudden sight of her, his horse reared and threw his rider to the ground. His left foot was in the stirrup, and the animal, now still more alarmed at the event, was dashing forward to the right through the forest, when Benita, with presence of mind, seized him by the bit and with great strength almost supernatural, restrained him, while she shrieked to her father for help.

Manuel flung down his glass and hastened with such good speed to her, that he came just in time to take the plunging horse by the head, when her courage and strength were failing her. He had already dragged his almost insensible rider as well as herself several yards ere Manuel reached the spot. He now grasped the bit with an iron hand, and with the other closely held his nostrils, while Benita, with ready self-possession, flew to disengage the foot of the horseman from the stirrup, which, being unable to do, she drew the fisherman's knife from her father's belt, and severed at a blow the stirrup's leather.

"Well done, brave girl," cried Manuel, letting the horse go, and hastening to raise the stranger from the ground. "You are not much hurt, I trust, senor?" he asked, as Robert Rosal with difficulty stood upon his feet.

"Only a little bruized, good Manuel!"

"Por Dios! It is master Rosal!"

"It is so, Manuel. I should have been dead master Rosal, but for the aid of thy brave daughter here, for such I doubt not she is, though I have never met her before!"

"Yes, and a good girl she is. Thanks to the saints that you are no worse hurt, sir!"

"I am so thankful, senor," exclaimed Benita, warmly, her fine face, on which the moonlight closely shone, flushed with the glow of her recent exertion to restrain the horse.

"I owe you my life, noble maiden," said Rosal. "At one moment I feared you would let him go. My heart was in my mouth. I was at the animal's mercy Manuel. I tried to raise myself from the ground to reach my foot, but in vain. The horse leaped forward madly. He lifted the fearless girl from her feet, yet she held firmly on. He tossed his head madly, and neighed with a fierce, hissing sound, he was so enraged. Then it was, I trembled, lest in her terror, she should give me up. I called to her to hold him a little longer, for I heard your steps vibrating along the ground. Thanks, both to thee, Manuel, and be assured—fairest of maidens—I shall never forget thee!"

"His very words," repeated Benita, in a half tone. "How strange."

"Let me lean upon thee, as I walk, senora! What is thy name?" he asked in in an under voice.

"Benita."

"Yes, so it is. I have heard of thee; but having been always from home, I have not met thee ere now. If I have my wish, it shall not be the last time. I must know, and learn to love one, to whom I owe my life!"

Benita trembled, and looked downward, and timidly gave him her hand to support his steps while Manuel hastened on before for a strengthening cup of wine.

CHAPTER VIII.

THE LUGGER AND BATTEAUX.

THIS wine will put new life into you, senor," said Manuel, reappearing from the cabin, and placing the glass in the hand of the injured horseman. "It will do every thing but mend broken bones."

The young man received it, and drank it off, though not without first looking

at Benita, and saluting her.   She was standing by the door at the side of which
he had seated himself upon a rude bench placed there.

"You say none too much in praise of your wine, Manuel," said Robert, returning the glass. "I feel my blood start again. I will be as sound as ever in a few
minutes."

"Empty another, master Robert," said the old man, going in to replenish the
cup.

"No, I shall require no more. Besides I have business on board."

"I should think it full pressing, the way you rode along the beach, and brought,
to as you were by a beamender!"

"That was this handsome maiden's fault, Manuel," answered Robert, smiling
as he glanced with admiration upon Benita, who was at his left. She was in the
path, as I rode up the bank, and my horse, unused to see angels in the way, became
frightened and threw me. If she had not, however, atoned for the mischief by
sezing him by the head, I had by this time been beyond the influence of thy good
wine, Manuel."

"I am sorry, sir, that I should have been the cause of your fall;" said Benita,
very sincerely.

"I am not. I would rather owe my life to thee than not. It has a new value
now."

He said this with a subdued tone, and at the same time took her hand and pressed it with warmth. She hastily withdrew it, and disappeared in the cabin.

"By the mass, Manuel, thou hast a rare jewel in thy home," said Robert, with
warmth.

"Yes, fair and good, fair and good, master Rosal. I would not give her for a
King's daughter, though I shall have but a few gold ounces to make her a fortune
out of. But how is it that I am honoured with a visit from thee. It is some ten
months since you came this way, and then in chase of a stag."

"Yes, and that stag led me many a mile along the lake shore after I passed thy
cabin, Manuel. If I ever come this way again, be sure it will be after a fawn—no
less a deer than thy daughter."

"This is too light talk young man, from thee to me !"

"Nay, I speak it gravely and with sincerity. Wilt thou believe me, Manuel,
when I say I have lost my heart to her this night."

"Then it were a heart easily lost, and often, and thou wilt soon find it. She is
not for one like thee to think of, Master Rosal. When Benita weds, it must be
with a poor, honest fellow, who is her equal. If thou hast other thoughts of her,
than those most honourable, breathe them not to me."

"Nay, I swear to thee, Manuel, thou dost mistake me. I am no man of pleasure
who, like the hawk, which banquets on doves, or the wolf on lambs, prowls after
innocent maidens to seek their ruin. I am a man of honour, Manuel. The good
service Benita has done me, has won my gratitude, and inspired me with love for
her. She is as beautiful as an houri. I care not for birth !"

"I know not the girl's mind touching thee," answered Manuel, "But I think
thou hadst best forget her, as surely thou wilt, ere three days pass."

"No, never. I owe her my life, and I will owe her my future happiness, by
sharing my life with her. Give me your consent, Manuel, to sound the maiden's
heart."

"There will be time when thou knowest her better, and she thee. Let us now
talk of what brought thee to my cabin."

"I had well nigh forgotten it. The presence of your daughter has made me
oblivious of every thing else. I will see her and thee further by-and-bye, touching
my passion.'

"The passion of five minutes intercourse by moonlight, cannot be very deep,"
answered Manuel, coldly. "So let it not take up our discourse at any time future.
To what circumstance am I indebted for the honour of this visit ?"

"You shall hear," answered Rosal, rising up and speaking with animation, all
his feelings of revenge against Louis having resumed their full force in his bosom,

extinguished even by love. "Come with me along the path. I can walk now very well. I know you are no friend to the revenue captain, Louis Dumont."

"Well," answered Manuel as they at length stopped by the lake.

"He is now on the lake in his boat. Doubtless he has been here as a spy, and contemplates some mischief to you. His boat is just visible in the distance. I wish to pursue him. He has dared to address my sister—nay—they are betrothed. I heard of it in Mexico, communicated to me there by some unknown friend. I hastened hither to stop the nuptials, and reached the villa to-night. I found the captain there holding an interview with my sister. I challenged him on the spot. My sister interposed. She managed to get my sword from me and cast it into the lake. He took this opportunity to fly to his boat near by, and escape me. I have galloped hither to fling gold into your cap if you will at once man a boat to pursue him."

This was spoken with fiery vehemence of feeling. His cheek glowed—his eye flashed—and his whole manner betrayed the most bitter vengeance.

"Why should not Louis Dumont wed Isabel Rosal?"

"Why? Do you not know that my father fell by the hand of his father. We are foes, he and I, by inheritance. If he crossed not my path I let him pass, and cared not to avenge my father's fall upon his head. But since he has dared to aim at an alliance with my sister—with the daughter of his father's victim, I shall not rest until we have crossed blades. This is my determination. He is now in his boat on the lake, and alone. He is in my power, so that you give me a boat at once to pursue him. Thou and I will be enough for this. You shall have gold at your wish."

"I have no small boat, master Rosal," answered Manuel, in the manner of one who felt quite indifferent whether he undertook the enterprise or not.

"I see two drawn up on the bank there."

"They are mere skiffs without sail."

"The wind is blowing fresh. Get your lugger under weigh. This is better than any other boat."

"I have no men with me, master Rosal."

"If report says truly, the blast of your horn will rouse half a score from the depths of the forest about your cabin. Come, come, Manuel—you must not say nay. What, are you so reluctant to overhaul and capture one of your greatest enemies?"

"Captain Louis never has yet troubled me, master. Besides, I don't much like to take even an enemy at disadvantage. It is not my way to come upon a man by surprise. I like to do, what I do, open and above board."

"And so do I. You mistake me in supposing I wish to take advantage of Dumont to capture him. I wish to cross weapons with him in fair fight. I wish to bring him before the point of my sword, where we can settle our feud. If I overtake him, I will fight him in his boat, breast to breast, and you shall look on and see that the combat is a fair one, Manuel!"

"Well, what gold will you place in my hand for this service—for my lugger and six men."

"Twenty ounces, if you overtake him, the half in your palm."

"Very good."

"But there is no need of so many men."

"Captain Louis is not alone in his boat. You may have seen him alone by the cliff, but he stopped by here and took on board four stout fellows of his own crew, whom he had left here to refresh themselves while he sculled alone up to the cliff!"

"You seem to be on friendly terms enough with these revenue men, Manuel, that you entertain them in this manner."

"I entertain all who pass this way and choose to leave silver for the wine they drink. I never ask what a man's profession is, so that his coin be current. His men came and went as I said, and he with them. So if you would pursue and overtake him, and bring him to combat, you must let me take a full crew."

"Well, as many as you will," answered Rosal. "If he escapes me to-night, I fear I shall not fall in with him again. My leave of absence from my vessel is already half expired, and I am resolved that he shall be put out of the conceit of marrying Isabel before I return to my brig."

"Bien! We will see. In twenty minutes I will be ready for you, master" answered Manuel, walking towards the edge of the bank where the lugger was secured, and commencing to haul her in to the shore by the line which held her. It was a large open boat with masts, of about ten tons capacity.

Rosal walked slowly towards the door of the cabin, and seeing a light hanging within, over the table, he entered. He looked round for Benita, who was seated by a low window, the reed shutter of which was thrown open, and looking out upon the lake, a glimpse of which was visible through the opening along which the path extended. She had closely been watching the movements of her father and his guest as they stood in the path.

As Rosal entered she rose with some embarrassment, and with native courtesy said,

"Be seated, senor. Are you better?'

"Much, indeed, I scarcely feel any of the effects of my accident," he answered, seating himself upon one end of the bench which was placed beneath the window. I cannot be satisfied, fair Benita, in cold thanks for the service you have done me; pray accept this little token of my gratitude."

As he spoke he removed from his little finger a brilliant diamond, and taking her hand, for she had risen and still stood by the bench near him, he would have placed it upon it.

"No senor" she said, smiling. "I have done nothing worthy of such a token. If I had not been in the path, your horse would not have thrown you. I have rather to apologise for the mischief I caused. I could not do otherwise than risk my life to save a life I had endangered. Keep your ring, senor."

As she spoke she disengaged her little hand from his hold, and with modest dignity stepped back a pace. Rosal, who was in every sense a gentleman, his only dark shade being his unforgiving feud against Louis Dumont, for his father's murder, as he chose to express it, was struck with this most becoming propriety in one whom, from the place in which he found her, he expected to find brusque and bold. He was pleased to find that she, to whom he felt he owed a debt of gratitude he could never pay, and who was so beautiful—so courageous, and who had almost captivated his heart, was almost modest and retiring. This discovery deeply interested him in her. His conduct towards her changed at once, and from treating her as the unbred handsome daughter of Manuel the fisherman he instinctively felt towards her the respect due to any young lady who might be an equal with his sister.

"She is as modest as she is singularly beautiful," were his thoughts. "Manuel said not too much in her praise. I will know her better, and if she prove to be as pure as she is fair, I will pay my debt of gratitude to her for saving my life, by making her my wife, that is, however, if she will not say me nay, as she might do; for she seems to have an independence of character about her that would prevent her from being dazzled by the offer of my hand. How beautiful she is! What eyes! What a perfect little figure! Cupid stole the shape of his bow from her lips without question. I am already ensnared. I tremble lest she should already have given her little heart away to some of those bold fishing lads of her class. But I trust not. Manuel has kept her as a choice jewel, and better knows her worth than to let her become a fisherman's drudging wife. He loves her too much for this. Heigho! I feel that my heart is no longer own. This was either a most fortunate or else unhappy fall of mine to-night!"

While these thoughts were passing through his mind, Benita was stealthily regarding him from beneath her drooping eye-lashes. She felt an interest, as it was natural, in one whom she felt her courage had saved from a dreadful death. He was, moreover, handsome, youthful, and seemed to think a great idea of the service she had done him. She felt the natural embarrassment of a young girl alone in the presence of a young man whose life she had saved and who she felt was regarding her with looks of mingled admiration and gratitude. We always like those we have saved. Benita, therefore, liked young Robert Rosal, and next to Louis felt that she should be more interrested in him than in any person in this world.

Robert was about to make some remark to her to break the silence that had befallen them both, when the voice of Manuel was heard without, and other voices in reply. Rosal started up and was going out, when Benita sprang towards him, and said eagerly:

"Where do you go to-night with my father?"

Before he could frame a reply, Manuel came to the door and said that the boat would soon be ready, as the men had arrived. Robert went out and beheld seven or eight men in three batteaux at the landing. In twenty minutes more the lugger with the whole party, Benita excepted, left the inlet and stretched away across the lake.

CHAPTER IX.

THE BARK AND ITS ADVENTURE.

THE lugger had no sooner departed on her enterprise than Benita ascended to the look-out to watch its progress. Her suspicions were excited by such a mysterious departure at that hour of the night. The question she had put to Robert Rosal he had not answered; and her father had been so busy with the men, that she had not an opportunity of learning from him its object. That it was not connected with the expected brig, she felt confident, because her father would never have taken a stranger with him on such an expedition. It was not until the lugger had got some distance out into the lake, that the truth flashed upon her mind.

"He pursues Louis!" she cried, with mingled surprise and alarm, "why have I been so dull? He has come hither to get a boat to pursue him! Oh, that I had known—that I had suspected this! The lugger pursues the same course he did, and seems to use every exertion to make progress! I see now through it all! Stupid and blind—if I had even suspected it, I would have used all my efforts to prevent it! Cannot I do it now?" she asked with quickness.

Once more she levelled the spy-glass at the lugger, and then searched closely in the distance for Louis' boat. But it had some time before sailed out of sight.

"He may escape! But I will not suffer Louis to be endangered, and endangered through me, too, without making an effort to save him from his enemy!—Yes, Robert Rosal is his foe, and it is I who have been the instrument in bringing him from Mexico and kindling the fire of resentment in his breast against Louis! Why did I not anticipate this result? Why, when I sent to him information of his sister's love, did I not foresee that he would destroy the lover in his anger? I have overdone my work—I see it all now. He has come hither and taken boat to pursue one whom I would loose my life to save. I will save him or perish with him. If my suspicions and fears are true, I may not be too late. Robert Rosal owes his life to me, and for my sake he will forego his purpose!"

How closely had the maiden guessed at the truth. What she did not suspect in the outset, suspicion now created in her mind and confirmed.

The sudden presence of Robert Rosal at the cabin surprised her, though she anticipated that he would return home from Mexico; for it was through her he had received intelligence that his sister was about to be married to Louis Dumont, and that his presence could only prevent it. She was not, therefore, surprised as her father was, to see him. But she did not once suspect the object of his visit to the cabin.   She at first believed that he had got knowledge of the source from whence the intelligence had come to him, and had visited her to question.   This idea filled her with shame and confusion while he was present.   Each moment she waited for him to speak to her on the subject, and she trembled at being questioned, lest he should discover the motive that had led her to take such a step.   She therefore kept reserved and out of his presence, and was glad to see him leave without questioning her.   She did not, from her fears for herself, once think that the preparations she saw going on had reference to Louis.   She looked upon them only as connected with the brig.   But when she saw Rosal enter the boat with the rest, and beheld it take its course across the lake in the very track taken by Louis's boat, then the truth flashed upon her mind, only to overwhelm her with grief.

She now acted with promptness and decision.   She left the look-out, hastened to the water-side, and launched a light skiff that lay partly upon the bank.   She placed in it two oars, and upon a third bound firmly, by two of its corners, her large scarlet mantilla, which she set upright to see if it would answer for a sail.

She then placed it on the seats, and taking the oars pulled out of the inlet into the lake.   After passing the drooping branches of the trees that concealed the entrance, she hoisted her little sail, and laying her course, she let the little bark go bounding away after the lugger, her heart throbbing with solicitude and hope.

The wind had by this time freshened, so that the waves broke about the prow in white caps, and there was every appearance that it would freshen to a brisk gale.   Still, unalarmed, she kept on rapidly leaving the dark shores.   The sail, however, being very low, did not sufficiently hold the wind, which with the strong land-ward tide, drifted her rapidly to the north and eastward along the shores of the lake.   She found that she was going as fast side-ways as forward, and that if she continued to progress in such a manner, she would loose the lugger altogether.   She therefore rigged a second sail out of her shawl, upon another oar.   This aided her for a few minutes, but a sudden freshening of the breeze carried it away, and the dashing waves tossed it, oar and all, beyond her reach.

She now tried to make her way along with the single sail, but the fastenings to this were shortly carried away, and it went flying through the air upon the wings of the wind, like a huge flamingo, with her pinions spread.   She clasped her hands in despair,

"Blessed Virgin, be thou there and save Louis!   Heaven is against me!"

Still she was not daunted.   She took down the oar, and with the other, which had hitherto served her as a rudder to steer the boat with, she commenced rowing.   But the tide was against her, and the wind by no means in her favour.   In a little while she looked up, and found herself close under a low cliff towards which for the last quarter of an hour she had been steadily drifting.   She saw at a glance that to attempt to get round the cliff and once more get an offing would be in vain.   Nevertheless she laboured hard at the oars; but where she made five feet forward, she was blown seven towards the land.   In despair she dropped her oars, and raising her clasped hands to Heaven, she strained her eyes in the direction in which she had last seen her lover's boat, and prayed with tears for his safety.

The prayer inspired hope.   Hope gave resolution and courage, and she once more resumed her oars.   But all in vain.   A heavy billow caught the little bark upon its shining bosom, and tossed it lightly upon the sands at the foot of the cliff.

She sprung out, and with the spy-glass in her hand, hastily climbed to the headland, that she might take a wider view of the lake, and see if the lugger was still in sight.   It was with tears, half blinding her beautiful eyes, and a heavy heart, and many bitter words of condemnation against herself, for not suspecting till so late, the dark purpose of Rosal, that she gained the top of the bank.

The moon, though it had sailed through three-fourths of its skyey voyage, was still shining brilliantly, and a broad beam, like a silvery cloud, fell upon the sward, through the branches of two noble trees that grew upon the cliff.

Benita stepped back with an exclamation of amazement and fear. Directly in the light of the moon-beam, her head pillowed upon a mossy root of the old oak, lay a maiden robed in white, her arm beneath her cheek, and her eyes closed in profound sleep!

Was it a vision? or was it a mortal form? She stopped and gazed intently

ROSAL SCRUTINIZING THE BEAUTY OF BENITA.

for a moment, and then coming nearer, she recognised the lovely countenance of one she had but twice or thrice seen in her life, Isabel Rosal!

She stood looking down upon that beautiful brow, and for the first time felt the sharpness of jealousy.

"So lovely! I wonder not that Louis hath loved her. Will he ever love more as he loved her? Alas, if he should scorn me, I have done all in vain. I have destroyed this fair girl's peace, and not secured my own. I will awaken her and speak to her. I can perhaps learn from her, whether her brother pursues Louis."

Benita bent down, and laid her hand softly upon the cheek of Isabel, and said in a low tone—

"Maiden, awake."

Isabel sprung to her feet and gazed upon Benita with bewildered surprise.

"Who are you? Certainly one so fair cannot be a messenger of evil?"

"I would not be, lady," answered Benita. "I am Benita, the daughter of Manuel the Fisherman."

"Yes, yes. I have before seen thee. What do you wish that you seek me here? The hour is towards the morning. I should be at home?"

"It is by accident that I meet you, lady," answered Benita. I was on the lake, in a boat. You see that the wind blows high, though the moon is dazzling bright. I was driven to land. Below there you see my boat upon the sands."

"I see it," answered Isabel, more assured; and approaching her with curiosity, she could not but admire her extreme beauty of face and grace of figure.

"You are then Manuel's daughter?" she said kindly. "I wonder that you should remain in such a rude manner of life—one so fair as thou art too!"

"He is my father, and it is my home. Home is dear to us all, however humble."

"True. I have often wished to see and speak with you. What were you doing at the lake? Were you fishing?"

"No, lady!" answered Benita with embarrassment.

"Have you been sailing far?"

"No. I embarked not half an hour since."

"Then you cannot have seen the boat. Yet you must have seen the lugger too."

"What boat, lady?" Benita, desiring to bring her out.

"Have you seen a lugger with many oars rowing on the lake? I fell asleep watching it, and it is no longer visible." And she vainly scanned the horizon of the lake in search of it.

"You will see it with the glass, lady," said Benita, who after discovering the lugger with it, handed it to Isabel and pointed out its direction from them.

"I see it now!" she answered. "But how odd. Do you always carry a spy-glass?"

"No, lady."

"You are almost a sailor, I fancy. I have heard that you go a fishing on the lake with your father!"

"Yes; it is my duty to aid him in getting a subsistence."

"Yours must be a strange life, Benita. Have you not a lover?'

"A lover, lady?"

"Bless me! Is it possible that you are so prettily ignorant of the term?—Have you no brave, fine young fisherman [that you dream about and prefer to any other person in the wide world?"

"All the young fishermen are alike to me, lady."

"Indeed. And you so pretty and only eighteen—certainly not eighteen. Can you read?"

"Read, lady?" repeated Benita, smiling.

"Yes, have you ever been to school, living in that wild place, and with such strange rude people?"

"I have an aunt in the city, with whom I have spent a great deal of time. She has taught me to read and write, and needle-work; and has besides given me a taste for books. I owe to her a great deal! She has taught me to be religious also, I am not wholly savage."

"Pardon me, then, for my impertinent inquiries, Benita. I conceived you must be quite ignorant ; yet your beauty and intelligent looks might have told me the contrary. We must be friends. You must come and see me."

" I will do so, lady, when I can leave my father. But I am unused to move out of my lowly sphere. I am too independant to be your dependant; and my habits have not fitted me to be your equal."

" I like this answer. It betrays character and proper spirit. Pray what we you doing in a boat alone on the lake to-night—and at so late an hour ? I confesre added the beautiful girl with a confidential smile, " that I have the greatest curir osity to know."

" Will you then tell me what you are doing, lady, at so late an hour, sleeping by the lake-side ?" asked Benita, archly.

" That I wont promise. Yet I do not see why I need conceal it from you, Benita. You seem to be so good that I can make you my confidant with perfect safety."

" I should be happy to learn the reason ; though it is possible that I may guess it."

" Guess it ?" repeated Isabel blushing deeply.

" Yes, lady. Was it not to watch the departure of Louis Dumont ?"

" You have well guessed. But what know you of Louis, or his departure ?— Have you seen him to-night ?" she quickly demanded.

" No, lady. I knew that he had been here and had left, and supposed you were here to watch his retiring sail.—Am I not right ?" asked Benita, with a smile.

CHAPTER X.

THE RIVALS.

ISABEL remained for a moment silent before answering the inquiry of the young girl, and then replied,

" Come, then, and sit by me, Benita, upon this gnarled root. I will tell thee truly why I am here, and thou shalt tell me also, wherefore you were abroad on the lake to-night."

" I will keep nothing from thee, lady."

" Then so much the better. Know then, Benita, that I have a lover. A lover is—for as you don't know I shall have to explain to you—a lover is a very handsome, noble young man, with fine eyes, a generous heart, and who thinks you the best and fairest person in all the world A lover sighs when he meets you, looks as bashful as a maiden when he is spoken to by you, and, and——'

" And becomes your slave, that he may by and by be your master "

" Who ever told you such things ?' exclaimed Isabel, startled, and looking with amazement upon the wild smuggler's daughter.

" My old Spanish aunt, Josefina."

" Well, all I have to say is, that she seems to have had expereince which you and I have not, and may better define a lover than I. So I will say no more on this score. I have a lover, but he is not one who will answer either to the definition of this aunt Josefina, or to any that I can give. He is quite above praise, Benita !"

" He must be a very good young man, then !"

" He is. He is all that is good and true. I have known him from a boy. We loved as children, and love now as lovers. But, alas, true love never yet ran smoothly ! Something always obstructs its placid and pleasant flow. My brother —have you ever seen my brother Robert, fair Benita ?"

" Yes, lady. He has passed our cabin while hunting.'

Benita thought she would not yet tell her that he had that very night been to see her father. She did not know what effect it might produce.

"He is a kind brother, save in one point. He loves not the one who loves me ! Unfortunately our fathers met in a fatal rencontre many years ago, and mine fell by the hand of my lover's father. This event has left a lasting inpression upon Robert's mind. He has never forgiven the son the father's act. He cannot, therefore, forgive him that he seeks my hand !"

"It is very natural, lady. I wonder that you can love him !"

"Do you wonder ? You would not if you knew the amiable character of Louis. His name is Louis—Louis Dumont !"

"Captain of the revenue cutter, Ringdove."

"Yes. Have you seen him ?"

"Once or twice, lady ! He is very noble-looking, and I wonder no more that you love him than I do that he loves you. Yet I should think that you would always have the remembrance of your father's dearh to chill your love !"

"It does not. He is innocent himself. My father was slain by the laws he had drawn up to regulate the duel. Louis is by no means to be responsible for his father's act, even were it otherwise. It would be ungenerous to suppose so for a moment."

"And your brother yet thinks so !"

"Yes. It seems natural, too, that he should have some feeling. Gentlemen look upon these things with very different eyes from what we do. 1 knew well that he would oppose our union. We, therefore, kept our purpose secret from him. But some enemy sent him intelligence, and to-night he arrived here in great anger, and chanced to come upon us when we were conversing together on this very spot. It was a most unfortunate meeting, and so unexpected, that we were taken quite by surp,ise. High words ensued, and they would have come to blows if I had not possessed myself of my brother's sword and cast it into the lake. Persuaded by me, Louis regained his boat and left the scene. I wonder who could be such an enemy to me or to Louis as to bring my brother whom I supposed in Mexico, thus suddenly and revengefully upon us to mar our happiness and shatter our hopes !"

"It may not have been an enemy," said Benita warmly.

"Who could it have been ? What motive could induce them to such a course? I do not know whom I have offended, that any one should thus envy my happiness."

"It may have been from different motives than any you imagine, lady," said Benita in as even a tone as she could command ; for she felt that her heart was throbbing with guilty agitation.

"I can conceive of none but malice or revenge !"

"And Louis escaped ! Wither !"

"He came in a small boat from his vessel, which was becalmed outside ; and after going down the lake to take on board his crew, which he left a little way up the shore, he set sail across the lake. It was at Manuel's, he said, he left them. Did you see him ?"

"1 was not at home. My father told me he had been there !"

"And that lugger which persued ?—Why have I not questioned you before ? Did not the lugger leave your father's in chase ?" she asked eagerly.

"Yes. such was my suspicion. It is now confirmed, lady, 'as it contaned your brother !"

"Robert ?"

"Yes, lady. He came there a little after midnight——"

"On horseback ?"

"Yes. He remained about an hour, and then left —th my father and half a zen or more men. They stood across the lake—and and——"

"And what ? I feared this. What more ?

"I then suspected that they were in chase of the boat in which the captain of the cutter had embarked, and fearing the worst, I embarked in pursui hoping, if

I overtook them, by my influence over your brother and my father, to prevent mischief."

"Your influence over my brother?" demanded Isabel quickly; "what debt does he owe to you? How is he bound to you?"

"He was thrown from his horse near the door of my father's cabin. I was near and seeing that his foot was lodged in the stirrup sprung to his aid. At the risk of my own life I saved him from being dragged a mangled corpse through the forests!"

"Did you this for my brother, Benita? Then be my sister;" cried Isabel, and throwing her arms about her, she warmly embraced her. "In saving Robert's life you have not only bound him to you but me also. Was he much hurt?"

"But slightly, though he at first seemed to be a good deal injured. But he soon recovered, and, as I said, shortly afterwards embarked with my father in the lugger."

"Brave girl!—and truly good reason had you to suppose that your influence over him might have deterred him from doing injury to Louis. I saw the lugger in chase, and feared that it contained Robert. And you put off alone in your boat, noble Benita?"

"I did. But as I had no other mast than an oar, no sail but my mantilla, and the wind being fresh, while the current flowed landward very strong, I could not shape my course: and after losing my mast I was driven upon this shore. I ascended the bank to see how the lugger was going when I beheld you asleep."

"I fell asleep watching the lake, I am filled with fear on Louis's account, after what you have told me. I wish you had prospered in your bold enterprise. Is it too late now? I will embark with you."

"We can do nothing, lady. The lugger is also out of sight. My only hope is that he may reach his vessel before they come up with him."

"Heaven grant it! Thy heart is oppressed at the sense of his peril. God forbid that Louis and my brother should ever meet! If they should Louis would fall, for he has promised he will never raise his hands against Robert, save in self-defence. What shall be done? But why are you so interested in Louis?"

This question was put abruptly, as if upon a sudden reflection. Benita dropped her eyes and it was some seconds before she replied,

"I did not wish bloodshed, lady!"

"But how came you to suspect that Robert pursued him? You could not have known of their hostile interview to night?"

"I did not."

"Nor of his hostility to my betrothed, because you could not have known it. It is very strange why you should have had any such suspicion; and then, without knowing Louis, to embark alone to save his life from Robert. What was Louis more to you than Robert?"

"I cannot explain all my impulses, lady," answered Benita, smiling. "See, the wind has lulled considerably. I must take my boat and return."

"Not yet. Let me look once more through your glass? It is possible that we may see the lugger returning."

"And you are right," answered Benita. "here it is to the leeward, on the left here, and easily seen without the aid of the glass. Look between the trunks of these two oaks?"

"Yes, I see it now plainly. Yet it may not be the same boat."

"Give me the glass, and I will at once ascertain?"

She placed the telescope to her eye, and after a moment's scrutiny, said decidedly,

"It is my father's boat. They return without having been able to overtake the cutter's boat."

"Are you sure of this? Oh! I could cry for very joy and gladness."

"How guilty I feel," replied Benita, "in having sought to destroy the happiness of this girl in severing her from Louis. Yet she loves him no more than I do. Nevertheless my heart smites me ; I am a robber. He is hers and not mine ! Oh, that I could forget him."

"What is that beyond the lugger ?" suddenly exclaimed Isabel, who still held the glass up to her eye.

"It is a vessel," cried Benita, with surprise, "and there is another to the windward of her. They are not five miles off ; we should have seen them before but for the branch of that tree. The wind and tide have kept them to the northward as they came into the lake."

"How much you seem to know about the sea, Benita. Can you tell me what the vessels are ?"

" Give me the glass, if you please ?"

The young girl looked through it a moment or two very attentively, and then said with a tone of pleasure.

"One of them is the Ringdove. The other, I can only guess who she is."

"The Ringdove ? Are you sure ?"

" Yes, lady, I cannot be mistaken in her."

" See, what is that ?" cried Isabel, starting. "Is it lightning ! Yes, there is the thunder peal following it. We are to have a storm."

" That lightning," said Benita, in an agitated voice, " is the flash of a gun on board the cutter, and the thunder its report."

"How fearful ! See ! There is another, and another. What can it mean ?"

" The other vessel answers back."

" It is the privateer which he has chased into the lake," said Isabel, greatly excited, and her fears aroused at the peril in which she saw Louis placed.

Benita said nothing. She eagerly watched the vessels ! The cause of this firing he well knew. She saw the other vessel was a brig, and guessed that it was the one which her father had been looking for. The cutter she saw had discovered her, and was endeavoring to bring her to. She now understood why the lugger had turned back, her father and Rosal having seen the cutter approaching. She felt thankful that her father was out of the reach of the firing, while her prayers went up side by side with those of Isabel, for Louis' safety.

The two vessels were now plainly visible. The moonlight shone brightly upon their sails. They were about four miles off. The cutter was farther out, and nearly astern of the brig ; while the lugger was about a mile and a half ahead of them, making for the land, and evidently anxious to escape from the danger behind. The cutter kept up a sharp cannonading for several minutes, which was responded to by the brig, while both vessels close-handed stood rapidly up the lake.

With the glass Benita watched every movement and reported them to Isabel who was too much excited to watch for herself, and closed her eyes at every flash of the distant cannonading.

CHAPTER XI.

THE CHASE.

WE will now follow Louis on his departure from the cabin of Manuel, the fisherman, to return across the lake to his vessel, which lay some miles off.—We have seen him, with the eyes of those who watched him, stretch across the lake and disappear in the hazy distance of the horizon.

The wind, which had at first been blowing a light four knot breeze, strengthed as he advanced, so that about the time he ceased to be visible to Isabel, as she watched him from the cliff, he found it necessary to take a reef in his little sail.

"If this wind holds twenty-four hours," he said to his men, "we shall be up with the Tortugas in that time, and perhaps fall in with the privateer thereabouts at once."

"It will be a feather in our caps, captain," answered the old seaman, who pulled at the after-oar, "if we can take that craft. They say she is a brig about two hundred ton, and draws twelve feet o' water for'ard, carries six six-pounders and a pivot gun amidships. This is what the men said as was in the schooner she boarded, and I talked with in Orleans."

"We shall be a match for her, my lads. The waves begin to grow large," he added, as one broke over the bows and drenched the men at the bow oars. "But we have only a couple of miles or so more to run. I can already see the little Ringdove ahead, laying to for us, and a signal light at her peak."

The men simultaneously turned their heads as they rowed, for they had taken their oars in the last twenty minutes, to help the boat to hold to windward, the tide setting very strong to leeward, and drifting them out of their course. The sight of the light, and the indistinct form of their vessel, inspired the seamen with new energy, and they made their boat bound over the waves with additional speed.

"That will do, my lads. We are far enough to windward now. Ship your oars, and take your rest. In twenty minutes we shall be on her deck."

"Sail, ho!" cried the old seaman, Ben Bulwark, to whom Louis had first spoken. "A sail dead aft, sir."

"It is a small boat, and at a great distance; probably a fisherman going out to his ground," responded the young officer, after looking back and standing watching for a moment the pursuing lugger, which was so far astern, that none but a seaman's practised eye could have distinguished it from the white caps of the breaking waves that intervened.

The boat dashed on her way for a few minutes longer under her reefed canvass, the four men seated quietly looking out forward, and Louis at the helm, sending his keen glances all around the horizon, and particularly along the opening, by which the lake communicated with the gulf without. He was in search of the smuggling brig. He had reason to believe, from all the facts which his spies, and and his own observations had gathered, that about this time the vessel with which he firmly believed Manuel to be connected, would appear off the coast. This idea was strengthened by the conduct of Manuel in his cabin, where he seemed to be impatient of the presence of himself and his men, and anxious to get rid of them, as if for a particular object.

There was nothing, however, to be seen of any other vessel, besides the Ringdove, which they at length approached, as she sat like an ivory palace of the sea—her white sails shining as bright as snow in the broad moonbeams.

"Boat, ahoy!" hailed a hoarse voice from the cutter's decks.

"Ringdove," responded Louis.

The shrill whistle of the boatswain now broke upon the stillness of the air, piping to the gangway, and the next moment Louis steered his boat alongside and sprang to the deck.

"What news, Gladson?" he asked of his first lieutenant who received him.

"Nothing, sir, save that we have got a good wind, and that I am glad you have got back; for we have been losing twelve miles every hour it has been blowing."

"Well, you shall not be detained a moment longer."

"Shall I make sail, sir?"

" Aye, at once."

The loud cheering voice of the officer was now heard resounding along the deck of the vessel, and the men, long impatient of the delay, sprung with alacrity to obey orders given out. In two minutes the sharp bows of the Ringdove were cleaving the waves, her top-gallant sails and royals were spread to the wind, and, like a race-horse given the rein, the graceful little armed schooner went bounding away in the direction of the wide waters of the Gulf.

Louis stood upon the quarter-deck, watching the proceeding of getting sail on his craft, and then calling for his spyglass he began to examine the horizon ahead with the keenest scrutiny.

" Nothing like a sail been seen, Gladson ?" he asked as he opened the glass.

" No, sir. We have kept sharp look-out."

Louis swept the surface of the lake about, and then recollecting the distant small sail he had seen astern when in the boat, he directed his glass in its direction. To his surprise he found that it was now distinctly visible, having advanced very rapidly, surpassing the speed of his own boat. He let his eye rest upon her for a few moments, and then directed the attention of Gladson to it.

" What do you make it out, sir !" asked the officer as he prepared to light a cigar at the binnacle lamp.

" A lugger. But what is strange it sails like an Italian polacca, and is rowed by at least half-a-dozen oars."

" It may be some boat connected with this smuggling vessel you expected about this time to be on the coast, sir."

" Possibly. Fishermen merely, don't go out with such a crew as she seems to have ; nor do they usually make such speed. The fellow is doing his best with sails and oars. Perhaps it is as you say. But touching this suspected vessel, my information is too vague to make any calculations upon."

" I thought, sir, you had certain intelligence that the last of this month a vessel would be sure to arrive from France or Portugal, laden with wine."

" What I heard was this. You know that last year when we discovered the empty casks, which were without Custom House brand, in the yard of Delaforme's stores, we were satisfied that smuggling was carried on. I resolved to go to the root of it. I paid spies, and finally, my information led me to suspect Manuel the Spaniard. So I paid him a visit, and the result proved to me that he was in some way concerned in the business. I at length, by a heavy bribe, corrupted one of the clerks at Delaformes, and from him learned that twice a year, for seven years past, a vessel loaded with wines had discharged her freight up the lake, and that it had been conveyed in batteaux by Manuel and his crew to the city, through a bayou, which has been long since supposed to be choked up and impassable."

" Yes, and doubtless it has been. I am sure that General Jackson had it filled up or its waters turned off, to keep the English from availing themselves of it to pounce upon the city."

" This clerk said that this vessel arrived every May and every October, towards the last of the mouth. On this information I resolved to give Manuel a call about this time ; when the order came for me to fit out and cruise after the Mexican privateer, I obeyed orders ; but I did not like to let Manuel go altogether, so I have been up to see how things look there."

" Killing two robins with one shaft, hey, sir ?" said old Gladson, a grey-headed hearty old lieutenaut of fifty-two.

" Yes," responded Louis, smiling. " I saw Isabel also."

" I guessed as much. But what did the Spaniard say at seeing you ?"

" He was civil and friendly ; but he seemed to be very anxious to get rid of me."

" Look here, sir," said the lieutenant with emphasis ; " I will forfeit my hopes of ever being an admiral, if I don't believe that this lugger is his, and that he is coming out to meet his vessel or look her up. I don't think it would be a bad move to let him come up with us and bring him to, and find out his business."

"It is possible. But see! He has fallen off from the wind; He is tacking and standing northward. He don't care to come nearer to us than he is. He looks suspicious."

"Bless me if it dosen't, sir! Suppose we give her a gun and bring her to!

THE CONFLICT BETWEEN THE MEXICAN BRIG AND THE RINGDOVE.

"She is out of range. Besides, we must make the best use of this fair wind to get to the eastward."

"True, sir. If the brig that this lugger seems to be after is ahead, we shall fall in with her."

"And there she is !" cried Louis suddenly.

Gladson directed his eyes in the direction in which his captain pointed, and saw not four miles off, ahead of them, and directly in their course, a vessel standing

No. 6.

in towards the entrance of the lake. Louis quickly placed his glass to his eye muttering,

"It is singular we did not see her before !"

"She has being laying her course directly for us, and in the rake of our eye. She has just squared away."

"No, she is tacking, See! She is scarcely visible again. She was going in stays when we discovered her. She has seen us and is running away. This looks suspicious !"

"Do you make her out to be a brig with the glass, sir ?"

"Yes, a brigantine—square forward and schooner aft. She answers exactly the description of the brig which was given me by the clerk.'

"Then let us give chase. A bird in the hand, sir, is worth two in the bush. This prize is in sight. We may never fall in with the Mexican."

"I think I will try to find out what she is," answered Louis. "Keep a couple of points nearer the wind, helmsman!"

"Aye, aye, sir!' responded old Bulwark, who had the wheel. The response was made with alacrity, as if he was alive to the new scenes opening before them. The men also flew round to brace up the yards with unusual activity ; and when, after a few moments, Louis gave an order for them to go to quarters, there was a shout which even discipline could not prevent.

"This is not a Mexican, my lads," said Louis, "that you are in such good spirits. It is a vessel suspected of smuggling. Unless I catch her in the act, or find that she has no regular papers, I can't touch her. But I hope we shall be able to make something out of her."

The Ringdove was about a league or little more astern of the chase, and by changing her course as she did, she stood directly after her. The lugger was also visible farther in the entrance to the lake, steering the same way with the two vessels, which was obliquely towards the opening to the lake. This opening was about four miles wide, and had a shore on the north and south sides —the entrance extending in a direction east and west. The two vessels were on the gulf side of the opening, but within a mile of it, and the lugger about two miles within the entrance, and the course of all three were northwest or nearly so, with the wind S. S. to half south, and blowing for the cutter an eleven knot breeze, though it was soon discernable that the chase did not make more than nine knots. When Louis discovered the brig, he was standing east by north, but after he began to alter his course, he continued to do so as the chase did, until both were steering northwest right towards the lake.

After running about twenty minutes, Louis, who had the wind of the stranger, and had forged ahead till when they entered the lake, he had got nearly abeam, all at once bore down for her to cut her off or else drive her ashore. The brig had no alternative but to stand right up the lake, for she had a lee shore on her starboard quarter. When Louis saw this, he exclaimed with exultation,

"She is taken in a trap. We shall catch her without fail. But I don't care to go up the lake again. Fire the starboard bow gun, Mr. Gladson, to see if she won't be good enough to come to !"

CHAPTER XII.

THE BATTLE ON THE LAKE.

THE smoke had hardly blown to leeward from the discharged six-pounder, when the gun was answered from the chase by one of heavier calibre, the sound of which was borne to their ears loudly against the wind.

"That was a twelve-pounder, sir," said Gladson,

"Yes. It sounded like one," answered Louis, surveying the brig through his glass. "See!" she fires again!"

While he was looking a flash lit up the chase, and the next moment a spent twelve pounder pounced in upon the deck of the cutter, and after staving in an harness cask, rolled harmlessly into the waste. Gladson ran and caught it up.

"This is a Mexican shot, sir. It has copper in it, mixed with the iron. I should'nt wonder if this was our privateer after all."

"It is not likely. This is the smuggling craft only, be assured. But we must return her fire with something better than our sixes, that wont reach half-way to her. When she hears 'old Jackson' speak she will know who she has to do with."

The eighteen pounder amidships was now brought to bear upon the brig, which was now about a mile and a half distant. The little vessel reeled and fearfully vibrated to her keel under its heavy discharge. The thunder-like sound sunk into the ears of the two maidens upon the cliff, and made them shudder involuntarily. It was heard by Manuel and Rosal in the lugger, and shewed them that the two vessels were becoming seriously engaged.

"Let us press all sail to the shore now that this revenue captain has escaped me," said Rosal. "I have no desire to be knocked over by shot from either vessel; and in a few minutes if we keep this course we shall be in the midst of their cross-fire. What brig is this?"

"It is more than I can tell," answered Manuel, who saw plainly that she was not his expected Portuguese vessel; for he had steered near to her, supposing her to be the smuggler nd intended to board her. But he saw that she was a smaller vessel and in all appearance quite a different class from the Portuguese; besides, he knew that she carried only a couple of six pounders, while he now heard firing and responding to the cutter's eighteen pounder with four or five twelves, and an eighteen pounder also. Manuel, therefore, was quite as desirous of keeping out of her way as Rosal himself.

For a few moments the two vessels kept up a very brisk firing, each instant drawing nigher to one another, for the chase had boldly hauled her wind and now steered so as to meet the advancing cutter, as if wholly without fear.

"The cutter has found her match," at length said Manuel, as the brig poured a whole broadside into the Ringdove at the distance of three-quarters of a mile. "That vessel is the Mexican privateer he has boasted he would capture. She has taken him all unawares in the net of his own words."

"Is it possible it is the Mexican?" exclaimed Rosal with animation. "If I thought so, and the cutter were only commanded by any other man than Louis Dumont, I would go back and help to defend her. As it is, I should be glad to have him fall into the Mexican's hands."

"You don't speak very patriotically, Master Robert. That is none of my affair. You may depend upon it that the vessel is the Mexican. She can't be any other; for there is no other craft in these waters that answers her description. See that! The cutter gets it heavily."

As he spoke, the eighteen pounder on board the brig was fired, and the shot carried away the fore-topmast of the revenue schooner.

"The cutter will be captured—that is certain," said Rosal. "She is crippled beyond escape."

"She does'nt seem to be trying to escape. She is standing right down for the brig with her remaining canvass. She means to board."

"Dumont is a brave fellow, there is no doubt of that," said Robert. "I wish any other man commanded his vessel, and I should be on her deck."

"Yes, he is a brave fellow. But we are better where we are," answered Manuel, who, disappointed in not seeing the Portuguese round, now believed that Pierre had taken the privateer for her, and so made his report. "It is my opinion the sooner we widen our distance between them the better. While we have been looking on, the two vessels have been forging their way, and we are now under their fire, if they choose to point their guns this way."

"They are too busy to think of us," said Robert, who, standing up in the ger, was watching the two vessels with deep interest. As a sailor and a naval officer, the whole affair was of the most absorbing character. Nothing but his deep hostility to Louis prevented him from urging Manuel to steer for the cutter, which was now less than a mile distant.

The chase was separated from Louis's vessel by less than half a mile, when the latter lost her fore-topmast, and this space was each moment diminishing. The Ringdove steered straight for the brigantine, firing every few seconds from her long gun, while the brig about once in a minute responded by a broadside, and kept close up to the wind, so as to meet her. It was the intention of Louis to board her. He had seen too late that he had become engaged with a very superior force, which could be none other than the Mexican privateer. The idea that it was the smuggler he did not entertain after her first broadside.

"We are fairly in for it now, Gladson," he said to his old lieutenant, "and we must do our best."

"Do you think it is the privateer, sir?" asked the officer, wiping from his forehead the sweat and powder; for he had been firing the long gun himself, not trusting anyone else to level it.

"Yes, how she came to cruise this way I can't imagine, unless in chase of the smuggling vessel I took her for. That vessel I believe is somewhere in our neighboured."

"It is likely, and accounts for her being here," answered Gladson. "We are unfortunate in losing our top-mast, sir. They fire their batteries confoundedly well."

"Yes, they have experienced gunners. Can't you give her another shot that will cripple her before we come down on her quarter?"

"I will try to do it," answered the lieutenant, going to his gun.

Louis himself took the wheel and steered the vessel. He was laying her course straight for the brig, and meant to lay the cutter along-side and carry her by boarding. It was his only alternative. The report of the eighteen pounder broke upon the air like a clap of thunder. Louis watched the result. A loud crash mingled with cries reached his ears; but to his disappointment the spars of the vessel remained standing.

"Never mind another shot, Gladson. Divide the men into two boarding parties. As I lay the cutter alongside, you lead one over the brig's bows, while I board her on the other quarter."

"Aye, aye, sir, we will be all ready for the word."

The cutter was swiftly coming down upon her antagonist, a little abaft her beam, so as to strike her quarter. The boarders with pikes and pistols took their posts, one half forward, and the other half on the quarter deck. The brig, seeing her approach, poured in a heavy fire of musketry. Many were killed and wounded upon the deck of the cutter, which nevertheless swooped swiftly down upon the foe, which being to leeward, was compelled to receive her.

When the Ringdove was about fifty yards off from her, Louis surrendered the helm to Ben Bulwark, and seizing his cutlass and placing a pair of pistols in his belt, he cried in a loud voice,

"Boarders, stand by!"

He was answered by a shout from his men fore and aft.

"Luff a little, Ben."

"Luff it is, sir."

"Steady, as you are!"

"Steady, sir!"

The next moment the cutter struck the brig heavily upon her larboard quarter, and then sliding forward, lay alongside, bow to bow. The grapnels were thrown and lodged upon the deck of the brig, from which came grapnels also, as if the enemy was as resolute as the cutter-men. Amid a close fire of musketry and pistols, Louis leaped upon the quarter-deck of the foe, followed by his party.

"Boarders away!" shouted Gladson from the bows, and led his men upon the bows of the brig through a cloud of smoke. In a few moments both vessels were enveloped in a sulphurous cloud, from which flashed a hundred pistols and guns and from which rose wildly and savagely the cries of combatants and the clangor of steel.

What a scene for the light of the calm moon to fall upon! Its pure beams could not penetrate the dark cloud of battle. We will not unveil the horrors of the scene by minuteness of detail.

The contest raged for seven or eight minutes, and the crew of the cutter was driven back to their vessel with the loss of half their number, Gladson severely wounded and their captain missing. The brig had proved too strong for them both in weight of metal and the number of men. They out-numbered those of the cutter two to one.

The second lieutenant of the cutter, who had been left in charge of her decks with about a dozen men, seeing how the fight was going, proceeded to separate the vessels when he found that his party was falling back upon the deck, and before the brig's crew could follow, the Ringdove swung clear, and aided by her sails forged ahead and out of reach of the boarders from the brig.

"The cutter has had the worst of it," said Manuel, who at a mile distant, in his lugger, was a spectator of the engagement, for the deep interest they all felt in it led them to delay, as it progressed, to see the result. "See, they have separated, and the cutter is escaping!"

"Yes, she flies. The brig opens upon her with her eighteens, and makes sail after her.

"And it is time we were escaping, too, master Robert. Did you hear that ball go whizzing through the air over our heads—not twenty feet high. It is time we were making for the shore."

The direction in which the shot was now fired, so as to reach the schooner, brought the lugger in range; and altho' they used sail and oar to widen the distance, the two vessels, coming on one after the other, kept it still under the brig's brisk fire. The schooner had got long musket-shot ahead of the brig, which was pressing all her canvass to overtake her, when an eighteen pound shot, passing over her, struck the water about forty yards from the lugger, rebounded, and lighted directly in the centre of the lugger, going out through her bottom. Those it had contained, and that were not killed by the shot, were at once cast upon the waves to buffet them for their lives. While they were struggling, the schooner, now become the pursued, passed within half cable's length, under every stitch of canvas, and sweeps out on both sides.

"Ho, the schooner," shouted Robert, who was with difficulty supporting himself by two oars, one under each arm. "Save us. We are perishing!"

"It is Manuel, Captain Louis!" cried the old Spaniard at the top of his lungs. "We have stove our boat and are sinking. Nombre de Dios, save me!"

The schooner passed swiftly by them at the distance of less than fifty yards. No reply was made save by one of the crew as she passed, who said—

"It is as much as we can do to save ourselves without stopping for drowing men."

Robert Rosal now gave himself up for lost. His only hope was in being picked up by the brig, which was rapidly approaching, every minute or two firing from one of her bow guns, the shot passing sometimes over their heads, and at others dashing them with spray.

"This is a serious night's work for us, master Robert," groaned Manuel. "My poor little Benita. She will die of grief, when she hears that I have perished. If she knew my danger she would be now praying for me to all the saints in Heaven."

"Do not despair yet, Manuel," said Robert with fortitude. "The brig will pass nearer to us and may take us on board. This is our only hope.'

"We shall be saved from drowning to be carried into a Mexican mine, to work in chains."

"We must run our chance, Manuel."

"If it is God's will, so be it," sighed the old Spaniard. "If we drown, shall you forgive Louis, for hatred of whom you brought yourself and me into this peril."

"I am not yet sure we shall die, Manuel. See, the brig is standing straight for us. Now shout with me!—Ho, the brig. Shout in Spanish!"

And Manuel obeyed his instructions in accents of despair.

CHAPTER XIII.

THE RANSOM.

THE brig was steering directly for the place in the water where Rosal and Manuel, with three of the lugger's crew were combatting the waves, and using every means to keep afloat. It came so direct that there was more danger that they would be run down and submerged by her, than seen.

"That shout is from the water," said the captain of the brig; "there are some of the schooner's crew overboard.—Every prisoner is of value. Stand by to heave ropes! No, lower a boat, for I see at least half a dozen heads darkening the surface, like so many buoys!—Luff a little, helmsman! Luff sharply! That is it!"

The brig by this manœuvre passed around to windward of the five men—her headway was a little checked—a boat was lowered, ropes thrown, and in two minutes they were all on board the Mexican.

"Who are you, and what is your rank on board the chase?" demanded the commander of the brig, as they were led aft to him; and seeing that Rosal looked like the superior, he addressed the inquiry to him.

"I am not an officer in the revenue vessel, sir," he answered; "but reside on the shores of the lake, and being abroad in a boat, a shot from your eighteen pounder stove the boat, and thus has placed me and my companions at your mercy!

"Are you not an officer?" demanded the Mexican, who was a young man of slight figure, with a moustache, fine dark eyes, and long, waving, coal-black locks. He had detected the naval buttons upon the vest of his prisoner.

"I am, senor."

"So I guessed. A lieutenant?"

"Si, senor, in the navy of the United States."

"Bueno. This is fortunate for us.—And you, senor?" he added, turning to Manuel.

"Un probre Americano—un piscador, senor," answered Manuel, dripping like a water-god.

"A Spaniard, I see. These are your fellows, I doubt not?"

"Si, senor escellenza."

"Bien. You are all my prisoners.—Don Diego, see that these four men are properly taken care of, and secured with the rest. Senor, I give you the liberty of the quarter-deck, in consideration of your rank."

"Gracias, senor," responded Robert, who saw that there was no alternative but submission to his destiny. Manuel was led away groaning at his fate, and talking bitterly about his fair daughter's sorrows when she should know of his capture.

"You have had the best of the conflict, senor," remarked Robert to the Mexican officer. "I see you are heavily metalled, and are numerously manned. Did not the cutter board you?"

"Yes. But we drove the crew back, when, before we could follow them to their decks, they cut clear, and made sail. But they left their captain, and nine men prisoners with us."

"Their captain!" exclaimed Rosal, with surprise.

"Yes. Yonder he stands by the capstan, with his arms folded upon his breast. He feels rather gloomy at his ill-fortune. But he is a brave fellow—He swooped down upon us from his bulwarks like an eagle. He fought like a lion, and yielded only to the last extremity. I respect a brave man, senor, even if an enemy. Would you like to speak with him ?"

"No," answered Rosal, with embarrassment. He was annoyed at this discovery. It made his situation as a prisoner more irksome and unendurable—He felt that he had really wronged Louis, and he did not like to be a fellow-prisoner with him—perhaps compelled to be together—share the same cabin.

The Mexican officer had not spoken too highly respecting Louis's conduct. He had, indeed, fought like a lion, and only when he saw that he had been completely deceived in the force of his enemy, which overwhelmed him with their numbers, did he give orders for his men to retreat again to the deck of the Ringdove. He remained last to cover the retreat of his men ; but remained only to fall into the hands of his foes. Struck with the courage of the prisoner, the Mexican captain, instead of ordering him below, gave him the courtesy of the deck. This courtesy Louis acknowledged with a suitable expression of thanks.

"You need not thank me for doing what your merit demands of me, senor," said the Mexican. "If I had fallen into your power I know you would have been equally courteous towards me. My countrymen have their reputation of acting towards our prisoners with the savage vindictiveness of savege tribes. It is my intention to convince you that we are injured in this opinion."

"I trust I shall find that you are, sir," responded Louis. "Will you tell me why you kept to the northward when I first discovered you, and thus led me to suppose you a merchant vessel ?"

"It was to escape being seen by you, I took you for a U. S. brig of war that has been the last three days in chase of me, and which I only lost sight of last night at dark, by running between the Chandeleur Islands and the main. To avoid her, I made for the lake, taking it for granted she would never search for me here. But as soon as you fired your six pounders, and I was enable to make you out clearly with my glass, I saw that you were a cutter. I then began to lay close to the wind for the purpose of bringing you to an engagement."

"I took you for a Portuguese brig that is suspected of being engaged in smuggling, or I should have calculated my chance better than thus to have come within range of your heavy guns. But when I once found that I was mistaken I resolved to carry you by boarding, as my only way of escaping capture myself. I was not however, sure that you were the Mexican privateer until I was near enough to discern the Mexican eagle and serpent painted on the glass of your battle-lanterns !"

"You have nothing to censure yourself for, senor, in having fallen into my hands. You did all a brave man could do !"

"I see you keep firmly at my poor cutter. Do you hope to capture her ?"

"I shall do my best," answered the young Mexican. "We have a small marine, and she will be of great service to us. She sails though like the wind. I can only hope to get her by disabling her. Yet I may run too close in with the land, heave the led there forward."

"Six fathoms," was the response of the leadsman, after a minute or two.

"What water does your schooner draw, Captain ?" asked the Mexican.

"Twelve feet."

"And I fourteen! I can't follow her if the water shoals much."

"And be assured it does, rapidly, captain," said Louis, anxious for the safety of his vessel.

"Quarter less four !" sung the leadsman from the fore-chains.

"You are right, senor. Stand by to put the brig about. We must give up the chase !"

" Three and a quarter fathom," shouted the helmsman.

" Ready about !" cried the Mexican captain in a quick startling tone. " The schooner is leading me into a snare. Hold ! What cries are these ?"

It was at this moment that the voice of Manuel reached his ears. The brig was, as we have said, then luffed up to take them on board, when filing away again for a few moments she went in stays and turned her stern in the direction of the schooner. One or two parting shots were fired at the cutter, and then the brig stretched away north and east across the lake towards the gulf.

Louis was standing by the capstain looking back at his schooner, which was rapidly receding in the distance. His grief at his own capture was greatly diminished by seeing her escape from his enemy's power. He had heard the shouts of Manuel from the water and recognised the voice ; and could not but wonder greatly how it was he was placed in such a situation. He saw him and Robert taken on board ; and not wishing to address the former he drew back to watch the result. He saw him led aft, and heard what passed between him and his captor. He heard even his refusal to speak with him.

" Poor Rosal ! He carries his revenge even to the remembrance of it in his own misery, when, if ever, a man needs friends and sympathy. I am sorry for his captivity ; but how is it that he was aboard on the lake ! Poor Isabel !— There is a deal of ill-news yet to reach thine ears ! I will speak with this Mexican touching our future disposal. It is possible I may get him to release Manuel, that I may send a message to Isabel, assuring her of my safety, though a captive. Otherwise all will be uncertainty, when she hears that my vessel comes back without me !"

Wih this resolution, Louis walked to where the Captain stood. As he approached him he had to pass Robert Rosal, to whom he bowed slightly and kindly. Robert only frowned and turned away his head.

" Senor captain " said Louis, with that frank and manly air which marked his bearing to friend or foe.

" Well, Senor captain Americano !" responded the little Mexican commander.

" As the fortune of war has thrown me into your power, I have seen enough of your civility to be convinced you will not increase the rigour of captivity by useless severity."

" Never, senor !" answered the Mexican with emphasis, and laying his hand upon his heart.

" Then I have a favour to ask of you, senor."

" Pray speak freely, captain !"

" If you will look in this direction you will see that the moonlight reveals the white walls of a villa about a league distant. In that villa dwells my betrothed bride. I wish to send word to her of my fate !"

" I should be happy to oblige you, senor,' answered the Mexican ; " but my safety renders it expedient that I should get into the gulf as soon as possible—The firing will have been heard by the U. S. brig, and she will be directed by it this way, although by my ruse I led her to suppose I had run westward to the Balize. If she should come off the mouth of the lake before I get out, I shall have to fight her, which I care not to do, as she is so much heavier than I am, being a larger sixteen-gun brig ! If I could serve you I would gladly do so, for I respect a brave man !"

" You can do so, senor. There is on board a Spanish fisherman, whom you took from the water. He dwells near the villa ; and, besides, he has a daughter very dear to him, who will greatly mourn her father's captivity. I am willing to pay this person's ransom if you set it within my ability, if you will allow him to return to the lake shore free !"

" I cannot do it, senor. I have no boat to spare !"

" As we coast along the entrance to the lake, you will find here and there, moored a few rods from the beach, a fisher's skiff. You can run near one of these, and let him jump into her as you pass !"

"If I can do this, I give my consent. The price of his ransom I will set at three hundred dollars. How can you pay it?"

"I have the sum in gold about my person," answered Louis, who had not only this amount, but quite two thousand dollars in eagles, concealed in a belt about his waist; and which he had placed there before he boarded the brig, lest, if, he should lose his schooner, this might fall to the enemy.

ROSAL OBJECTS TO SHARE THE SAME CELL WITH LOUIS.

"Very well, senor? entrust the Spaniard with your message. Don Pedro," he added to a junior officer, "lead hither the old man we picked out of the water." In a few moments Manuel was brought before the Mexican.

"So, hombre, you are a fisherman!" said the captain.

"Si, senor."

"This officer has begged of me your liberty. I have fixed your ransom at three hundred dollars!"

"No es possible for me to pay it, senor excellenza!"

"Don Louis, here, pays it! He wishes to send a message on shore by you!"

No. 7.

"Thanks Captain Louis! My poor child will bless you!" cried the grateful Manuel.

"There is the gold, senor!" said Louis, counting out the money upon the top of the companion way.

"Gracias, senor. I receive this for my crew, not for myself. We are approaching the land. As soon as I see a boat he shall be left in it. Now deliver to him thy orders."

With these words the Mexican walked aft to give directions to the helmsman.

———

CHAPTER XIV.

THE MEXICAN AND HIS PRISONERS.

Louis took Manuel aside, Robert following their movements with his eyes; for he had overheard and witnessed what had passed, and well knew that it was his intention to send word to Isabel touching his fate. Gladly would he have added something himself to Manuel's errand, but his pride and hatred prevented him from it. He, therefore, stood and watched them with a sort of gloomy ferocity. If he could have done so, with any power to prevent it, he would have interposed to stop the message from the lover to his mistress.

"Now, Manuel, that I have ransomed you, I hope you will do me good service," said Louis.

"I will do whatever you say, master Louis," answered the grateful Spaniard.

"I wish you, as soon as you land, to hasten to Isabel, and inform her of what has occurred, and of my situation, and that of her brother. Tell her that it is probable we shall be taken to Vera Cruz, as prisoners of war, and there detained till we are exchanged or ransomed; for the Mexican privateersmen receive ransom for their captives."

"I will tell her, captain. But this has been a bad night for you, as well as me. I have lost my lugger and some of my men, but this is not worth talking about now your goodness has made me free; and especially when I think of your loss. How am I to be landed?"

"The brig will run nigh some one of the fishing skiffs that their owners moor from their huts. You will jump into one as we pass, and make the best of your way to the villa."

"I will do it, senor. How Benita will bless, and pray for you, for saving me from a Mexican prison. It would have fared worse with me, senor, than with you; for you are officers, and will have the best of treatment. I will also repay you the sum you have paid by and by, if you are ever sent home free. I wish I could help you to escape, sir."

"You can do nothing, Manuel. But, I have another message for you to deliver. I want you to board the cutter, and see Lieutenant Gladson, and tell him that I am a prisoner, and well, and that I shall probably be taken into Vera Cruz. Tell him that the brig carries ten guns, (twelves) and an eighteen pounder pivot gun, and is manned with a resolute crew of ninety men; that they lost but eleven in the engagement. Tell him that we are standing out into the Gulf; and that the Mexican captain was chased in here, by a U. S. brig of sixteen guns, that is now not far off. Therefore, say to Gladson, that he must get repaired as soon as possible, and sail out of the Lake, and try and fall in with the U. S. vessel, and report my capture, and that the Mexican brig will steer, as I overheard her captain say, for Vera Cruz. This will show him in what direction to give chase.

But tell Gladson not to think of pursuing us with the cutter, or he may lose her as well as her captain."

" I will report all this, accurately, master Louis," answered Manuel.

" Stand by, there, sir Spaniard," cried the captain. " There is a skiff just ahead ! Be ready to jump into her. Take an oar in your hand, for there may be none in it."

" Now remember my messages, Manuel," said Louis, given him his hand. " And here, take this ring, and from me, place it on Isabel's hand."

He removed it, and was putting it in Manuel's hand, when Robert Rosal, who saw and heard all distinctly, as he was not three paces off, strode up and struck the hand Manuel held out to receive the ring. The ring flew into the air and fell glittering into the water. Louis would have levelled a blow at his breast, for this brutal act, but, remembering Isabel, he forbore to strike the brother. He said, merely—

" You know, sir, why I forebear,"

" What means this ! caballeros ? Senor, I will not allow insults. Stand back," cried the Mexican, sternly addressing Robert. " What means that blow ?"

" I will tell you, senor," answered Manuel. " These two gentlemen were once the best of friends. They are now unhappily foes. This noble captain is betrothed to the sister of the other. The sister loves—the brother hates ! I am to bear a message from the lover to her, and with it he placed in my hand a ring, to be placed upon her finger. Seeing this, the brother struck up my hand, and tossed the ring into the sea ! And, to make a long story brief, I will tell Mr. Louis, that what brought me out upon the water to-night, was a large reward from Master Robert, if I would launch my boat, and try to overtake you, sir. He said he wished to cross blades with you, and punish you for thinking of Miss Isabel as your wife. It was this that got me in the way of the flying shot, and lost me my lugger, and nearly my life. I am sorry now, Master Louis, that I should have taken wages to pursue you; but I intended you no harm. Master Robert here, said he only wished to come up with you, before you got to your schooner, that he might bring you to single combat. He had no other intention, nor had I any purpose, save to put into my purse the gold he offered me."

" The skiff is close alongside," shouted the officer of the deck.

" Spring, Manuel," cried Louis, grasping his hand. " I do not blame you for your part. Forgot nothing I have said to you."

" Not a word. Beware of Robert Rosal," he added in a whisper to him, as he cast himself over the side, and dropped into the little skiff, that the brig just grazed.

Louis looked over the quarter at him, as the boat faded in the distance, saw him take to his oars and pull in the direction of the villa. He then turned away with a sigh, and with a prayer that Isabel might be sustained under the heavy intelligence, she was about to receive from his lips.

" Now, senor," said the captain of the Mexican, if you tell me to put this person in irons for his insult to you, I will do it. It was a base act, his tossing the ring into the water in that fashion !"

" No. Do not take any notice of it, captain. I assure you he is a noble gentleman, though something strong in his hatred towards me. Besides, I do not wish to have any one interfere in our feud, save as a mediator."

" Can I be this ?" asked the polite Mexican.

" Ask him," answered Louis, and, if you please, you may assure him that nothing would give me greater happiness than to be friends with him, especially under the circumstances in which we now find ourselves placed !"

This was spoken with the frank cordiality of Louis's character. Captain Mejia advanced to the other side of the deck, where Robert was pacing up and down in gloomy silence.

" Senor," said the Mexican, " I have seen with regret your insult, given upon my quarter deck, to a gentleman, who, like yourself, is my prisoner, and under my protection. I have asked the officer if he desires to have you put in security where you cannot enact further violence upon him."

"And doubtless he answered you, that he would be extremely obliged to you, to put irons upon me. There are my wrists, iron them."

And Rosal stretched out his hands with an air of defiance and contempt.

"You mistake him, senor. He said I should offend him by such a step, and he desired that if I interposed in any way in the matter between you, it might be as a pacificator. This I wish to be, senor. I see that you are both noble gentlemen, and only a slight cause of difference exists between you. He has authorized me to say that nothing would give him so much pleasure as to be reconciled to you!"

"I dare swear it. He loves my sister, and therefore, would pacify me!"

"And wherefore should he not love her, senor?" asked the Mexican captain, smiling. "He seems to be a caballero that would well please a lady."

"His loving my sister, senor, is not by any means the ground of our quarrel!"

"Then pray may I know what is it? For by San Diego, I would fain make up your quarrel; for I mean you shall both be my guests in the cabin, and it would be an ill-matched company to have two hostile at my board."

"Senor, that officer's father slew my own unfairly in a duel. This is the cause of my dislike to him. Seek not to remove it! Make no effort to reconcile me to him. I can never look upon him but with detestion. If I grasped his hand in amity, I should look to see my father's ghost stand menacing before me."

"This I see is no matter for my mediation," muttered the Mexican, recrossing the deck. "Senor," he said, addressing Louis; "I have spoken with the gentleman, for I fain would have you friends; but he says that reconciliation is impossible, on the ground that your father took the life of his. Is this so? If it be, it is most unfortunate."

'It is true, senor; though it was in a fair contest. He thinks it his duty to avenge him on me."

"And yet the lady, his sister, does not share in the same spirit of unforgiveness, but the contrary, is it not?"

"It is, captain."

"For her sake and thee, I would have done something with him; but he is as morose as a bear. I could do nothing."

"I regret it. Reconciliation is] impossible, I fear. Towards him I have no hatred; but rather, for his sister's sake, love him."

"And he hates thee heartily. I will take care that he does not do thee a mischief on board."

"Do not restrain his liberty, captain. I do not fear any secret attack."

"Secret? Who accuses Robert Rosal of attacking his enemy in secret?" haughtily demanded the young man, crossing the deck to the spot where they stood. "You need not fear me, Louis, I am an open foe, as thou knowest, and every where thy foe. Blood only can wipe out the quarrel between us. Captain Mejia, if you would see this difference settled, place good swords in our hands, allow us six feet of the deck, and if Louis Dumont dare meet my challenge, which I now give him, I will soon end this feud."

"Nay, senor, I could not consent to this. You are the prisoners and property of Mexico; and I can't run the risk of losing you, one or both, with a sword thrust. No, no. I must look carefully after you both; for your lives are worth the lives of two Mexican officers of equal rank, prisoners with the Americans. Unless, senor Rosal, you pledge me your parole of honour that you will not seek to pursue your quarrel with this officer, I shall feel it my duty to place you in confinement."

"I have no desire to assassinate him. I am not a murderer as his father was."

The blood leaped to Louis' cheek, and he made a step forward, as if to strike him down; but the face of Isabel rose up before his eyes, eloquently pleading for her brother, and he restrained the impetuosity of his insulted spirit, though it cost him a strong effort. Captain Mejia seeing that it would be impossible to unite two elements so discordant as the tempers of his prisoners, resolved to separate them. He ordered Rosal to be placed in a state-room and confined to it, while he offered to Louis a share of his own cabin and table, as the brave commander of the vessel which had engaged him.

"Sail, ho!" was now called by the man aloft, in a loud, startling tone.

"Where away?"

"To the southward, about S. S. E.

"It is a large square rigged vessel," said the captain, putting his glass to his eye. "It is, doubtless, the brig of war! Have the decks all cleared, and the call beat to quarters?"

The order was received with alacrity by his officers and crew, while the Mexican, fully aware of his danger, kept away as much as he could, to widen the distance between him and his adversary.

CHAPTER XV.

THE PRIZE AND THE GUN-BRIG.

THE day now began to dawn, and with the increasing light the Mexican discovered that the stranger was a large brig-of-war, as he had anticipated. She was now standing directly for them, crowding all sail to get through the channel.

"A sail on the larboard bow!" shouted a man from the fore-top.

"Ha! What can this new vessel be?" cried Captain Mejia.

He went into the waist so as to get a clear view of her, and with his naked eye discerned a vessel nearly ahead of them, about six miles distant, and hugging the northern shore as closely as possible; indeed she was so close in under the land, that it was with difficulty she could at first be made out; but when once seen was easily ascertained to be a vessel standing west, in the direction of the entrance to Lake Borgne.

"It is my opinion that brig is a smuggler, that I have been told was expected on the coast," said Louis. "I wish you would keep away a couple of points, senor, so as to meet her. If she is the brig I fancy she is, you will get a rich prize."

"What is her nation?"

"Portuguese; but she always sails under the American flag."

"I will try and see what I can make of her. I shall run away from the gun-brig quite as fast by altering my course to meet this vessel; and if she hoists the Yankee flag, I don't know but that I may stop long enough to board her."

The privateer now altered her course a little, and stood on so that the two vessels would meet as the other was then running. But no sooner did the other see this movement than she suddenly tacked and ran eastward, spreading all her light sail, and even adding lower studding sails to effect her escape. Upon this the privateer crowded canvass after her, and the brig of war astern pressed closely upon her heels. The privateer at length gained upon the chace, and after two hours came up within range and fired a raking shot to bring her to, or make her show her colours.

She immediately ran up the American flag, but still kept on in her efforts to get away. The privateer gained on her each moment, and after firing three more shots at her, one of which cut off her mainmast twenty feet from her deck, the chace lowered her flag and hove to.

"I beg of you, senor," said Louis, as the Mexican Captain was about to step into his boat to go on board of his prize, "I beg that you will permit me to accompany you. I am very desirous of ascertaining the facts about this vessel and her smuggling operations; for she is, no doubt, the brig I have been looking for!"

"You shall accompany me, if you wish, senor," answered Captain Mejia, making a gesture with his hand for him to pass over the side into his gig.

In a few minutes they were along side the prize, which was a rusty, old Portuguese brig, that looked as if it might have been one of the fleet of Columbus. She had four ports to a side, but there were but two six-pounders run out of them; the rest being wooden guns. There were about twenty dirty, red-capped looking rascals on board, who, with their captain, were looking curiously over the bulwarks at the Mexican, as he came alongside. A rope was thrown to the gig, and the boat alongside.

"What brig is this!" demanded captain Mejia, of a short, fat man, his face half hid in enormous red whiskers, who held a speaking trumpet in his hand, and came to the gang-way to receive them.

"The Don Pedro, of Lisbon," answered the burly Portuguese. "What vessel are you, that you fire upon, and board a peaceable merchantman in this fashion?"

"I am a Mexican privateer. I capture you as a fair prize, sailing under the American flag."

Upon hearing this, the Portuguese looked amazed. He stammered as if he wished to ask a question, but feared the reply. At length he said,

"Is it possible the United States and Mexico are at war?"

'Yes. Matamoras is already in the hands of General Taylor, of the American army."

"Por Dios! Then I am a lost man! If I had hoisted my own flag I should have been safe."

The poor captain walked and stared round, swearing terribly. He felt there was no remedy; that he had been taken in a snare of his own device.

"Be peaceable, signor," said the Mexican. "You had best make the best of it. Give me your gold and silver, and some dozens of your best wine, and I will let you go; for to tell you the truth, there is a customer behind, who, I have no desire to come any nearer than he is. Be diligent and honest. Get your gold and silver on deck, and have it conveyed into the boat. You must have at least, ten thousand dollars. Your wine-ships always carry coin to buy return cargoes with, over and above what your wine sells for. Be quick, or I will return on board my brig and sink you with a broadside."

The Portuguese glanced at the privateer brig, which was lying to, within pistol shot of him, her tiers of guns looking menacingly towards his devoted vessel, and then, with a woful visage, gave the necessary orders to his crew, going into the cabin with them. The Mexican followed him below, while Louis remained on deck; and, seeing the mate near him, he asked him if he was not bound in to Lake Borgne when he first saw the privateer. The mate looked surprised; but when Louis pressed him closely, and showed so much knowledge of his business, he confessed it; and, also, that Manuel was the agent to whom the freight was to have been delivered.

"All this I knew, and, it has been my wish, (for I am a revenue officer) to fall in with you," said Louis; "but I am now a prisoner, and can do nothing. You will be released as soon as the Mexican gets from you what money you have on board; and as, no doubt, you will yet fulfil your intention of going up the lake, I wish you would inform Manuel where you saw me, and that I have my parole, and am well treated, and that Robert is also well; and that we are being chased by a U. S. brig of war, which will not, however, be likely to overtake us, we sail so much faster than she. Tell him to communicate these facts to the person to whom he formerly had an errand."

"I will do it, sir," answered the mate, very civilly; for he was agreeably impressed by the frank, sailor-like manner of Louis. He then gave him a full account of the system of smuggling which had been pursued, and in which, this vessel had been an instrument, thinking, no doubt, now that the revenue officer was a prisoner, that it could do no harm.

Louis did not inform him that the cutter was still up the lake, being secretly in hopes that the brig might fall into its power.

The Portuguese captain, with many groans, and huge oaths, saw the privateer's boat quit the side of his vessel with four boxes of silver coin, and three bags of gold, in all, seventeen thousand dollars. This prize put the privateer's crew into the best humour, and they willingly made sail again, leaving the brig to go her own course. To have taken possession of her they knew would be only to lose her again, to the U.S. brig astern, and to endanger their own safety. Captain Mejia at once divided the money among his men ; and then made them a short speech, saying, that as the brig of war was in chase of them, their escape would depend on the skill with which the vessel was managed, and he hoped that every order would be obeyed with alacrity ; for if they were taken by the brig, a prison would be their fate.

" At to fighting the gun-brig, we can't think of such a thing, my lads," said he in conclusion of his address to them ; " she is twice our force, and then there is no prize money to be got by it. Our course is to show her a clean pair of heels. But if she overhauls us, I shall not surrender without a fight ; and in this case I know and feel that each one of you will do your duty to a man."

This address was received with acclamations, and the brig once more got under a crowd of sail and stood eastward. The Portuguese was still lying to where she had been left, engaged in repairing damages as well as could be done.—Having but one mast, she could only move with her head sails ; and to enable her to lay her course, they commenced rigging a jury mast on which to hoist the trysail.

" That fellow will lay there," said captain Mejia, " until the brig of war comes up where he is, and then he will tell his story and also make known to her captain just our force."

" You would be a strong antagonist for the brig, captain," said Louis.

" Yes ; but I am a privateer and not a vessel-of-war, and in fighting with a gun brig I should get more iron than gold. It is my business to keep out of the way of such company. My profession is to board merchantmen and to capture rich prizes. I should never hope to take the brig, and there would be no glory in a fight with her. No, my only course is to run away !"

And swiftly was she running from her enemy, with royals set and starboard studdingsails alow and aloft, she dashed gallantly over the light green waters of the Gulf, evidently widening each moment the distance between her and the vessel in chase.

In about thirty minutes after the privateer left the Portuguese vessel, the gun-brig came up with her and after laying to for about three minutes under her quarter, made sail again after the Mexican.§

" She has heard the story of the poor fat captain, and knows too just what we are," said Mejia. " She will now be more anxious than ever to overhaul us ; and our anxiety to escape must be proportionably increased !"

The privateer now got an offing so wide that she altered her course and run more southwardly. Every hour the brig of war lessened in the distance : and by noon her topsails were even with the horizon. By night she was out of sight ; and six days afterwards the privateer came in sight of the blockading squadron, under Commodore Connor, off Vera Cruz.

CHAPTER XVI.

RUNNING THE GAUNTLET.

The presence of the fleet off Vera Cruz, was an obstacle that the genius of Captain Mejia was now called upon to overcome. For this purpose he resolved to stand off until dark, and under cover of the night run into the harbour, every fathom of which he was perfectly familiar with.

He therefore had no sooner made the lower main upon which Vera Cruz stood, than he bore sea-ward again, until the lofty snow summit of the Perote-peak sunk to a level with the horizon. But no sooner had he given orders to tack, and stand towards the port, which he had made his calculations to reach about midnight, than with his glass he discovered a dark object on the verge of the sky and water, that looked like a rock suddenly arisen from the sea. It was at a great distance, full fifteen miles off, and for some minutes he could make nothing of it. But he soon was satisfied that she was in motion towards him. It was now clearly perceived to be a vessel, but it appeared to be one at anchor, for not a stitch of canvass was visible. But a little clearer observation showed the Mexican, that so far from being at anchor, it was approaching him at the rate of twelve miles an hour.

"It is the Princeton steamer," cried Louis, as he took the glass. "You are captured, captain, without hope of escape. She has seen you when you were off the port, and having got up steam, is now stretching towards you like a hawk after its prey!"

"I see how it is, now," answered Mejia. "My only chance is to fly for it till night, and then do my best to get under the land!"

And he did fly for it! His vessel was put away before the wind, and went bowling off at the rate of ten knots an hour directly east. Night came on and found the Princeton within five miles of her, and gaining steadily and rapidly. Darkness had no sooner shut her out, than Mejia gave orders to tack ship. The Princeton in a few minutes more, was bounding away in the direction of Vera Cruz. She continued this course for about twenty minutes, when the captain suddenly gave orders to furl every stitch of canvass. Scarcely had the order been executed ere the steamer, whose light had been all the while visible ahead, and seemingly very near, went steaming past them, not half a mile distant. The privateer remained motionless upon the water, until the steamer had passed full a league to leeward, when the clear voice of her captain rung throughout her decks.

"All hands to make sail! Lively, men!"

"That was a masterly manœuvre, captain," said Louis, who had witnessed the result with mingled surprise and disappointment. "I had made up my mind to be a free man again, in another half hour, when I saw you put back and lay your course directly in the track of the pursuing steamer!"

"I had made my calculation, and, as you have seen, with success. By taking in sail I knew she could not see me in the dark, at the distance she would pass. If I had stood or had delayed half an hour till the moon rose, I should have been either overtaken or seen. As it is I am now safe. Before morning I shall be snug in Vera Cruz!"

The Mexican captain was not wrong in his anticipations. He made the lights of the blockading fleet off the Castle of San Juan de Ulloa at eleven o'clock, and immediately shortened sail by taking in everything but his trysail and jib, so as to present to the eye as small a surface as was possible. He stood on boldly. Not a light was permitted on board, not even in a binnacle. The wind enabled him to keep well to the northward, and as the positions of the several vessels of war were easily made out from the lights which hung in their rigging, he was able to avoid them. By keeping to windward, and running into shoal water, he was enabled to reach the Sacrificos without detection. Here a small schooner of war, which had been running in towards the castle to reconnoitre, came near him; but probably snpposing the privateer to be one of the blockading vessels, it tacked soon after it was discovered, and stood southwardly. This left the way clear, and in half an hour more, the Mexican was safely anchored under the walls of San Juan de Ulloa.

ESCAPE OF THE PRISONERS FROM THE CASTLE.

Louis who had been on deck during the whole of this bold enterprise of running the blockade, now could not refuse expressing to the captain his admiration of his skill and daring; albeit, through them he had been openly brought into Vera Cruz a prisoner.

He now looked up to the walls of the strong fortress, the artificial Gibralter of the West, and gazed upon them with amazement. They seemed to express with wonderful power the majesty and strength of war.

The dawn broke and showed him the town of Vera Cruz on his left, the castle on his right and in the distance the American squadron.

No. 8.

" I suppose you are quite disappointed, senior," said captain Mejia to Louis, "in not being on board one of those vessels this morning."

" I assure you I am. I had no idea you could get into the harbour."

" No one unless perfectly familiar with the navigation of its entrance could have done so. Besides it was in the night. I had reduced my canvass till hardly anything was seen above deck but the spars, and passed in by a channel little used. Here comes senor Rosal. I have sent for him to see if he is disposed to be friends with you, now that you are likely to be fellow-prisoners. Good morning, senor," he said to Robert, who, pale and stern, was now conducted by an officer to the place where they stood. He suddenly stopped and cast his eyes round him with surprise.

" Are we in Vera Cruz harbour?" he exclaimed with an astonishment that seemed to absorb every other feeling.

" You have guessed right, senior," answered captain Mejia, smiling, as he saw him stare about him, now at the city, now at the frowning walls of the castle.

" Then my hopes of recapture are overthrown. Have you come in, senior captain, in sight of the squadron?"

" No, senior. Not in sight of it, for it did not see me ; or if it did, took me for one of its own vessels. I am glad to welcome you to Vera Cruz. Yonder is your prison," added the Mexican, " and as you are likely to share it with Captain Louis Dumont here, I would recommend to you to bury all differences and be friends."

Robert replied only with a haughty, defying glance at Louis, and then turning away his head, seemed to wish to insult him by his disdain. Louis merely smiled. The recollection, which never left him, that it was Isabel's brother, prevented him from feeling resentment.

" Very well, senior, I have done my part. I must now deliver you to the authorities, who are coming on board in the boat which has just put off from the castle stairs."

The barge which was rowed by twelve soldiers in green jackets and red trowsers now came alongside, and a tall officer in gold and blue, accompanied by two very handsome young men, richly dressed in superb uniforms, came upon the deck. Captain Mejia seemed well known to him, and the other two having shaken hands, a conversation took place aside, which resulted in the officer's being presented to each of the young Americans.

" It is the fortune of war, Caballeros," he said. " You are now under my protection and care. You will oblige me by going into the boat."

Louis obeyed, though Captain Mejia first shook him warmly by the hand, and said he hoped he would speedily be exchanged. Robert also went into the boat, refusing even to acknowledge the Mexican's " adios," and taking a seat opposite Louis, he amused himself by watching the waving of the gay Mexican flag, as it rose to the staff-head and caught the beams of the rising sun. The sun-rise gun at the same moment thundered from the battlements, and was heard simultaneously from the fleet,

" Adios, Caballeros," cried Mejia as the barge pulled off from the vessel : and watching it he saw it reach the castle stairs, and his late prisoners disembark, and guarded by a file of soldiers, disappear in a gate near one of the bastions.

" Now, caballeros," said the governor of the castle, before whom the prisoners were conducted soon after their entrance beneath the walls of the castle ; " now, if you will give me your parole never to serve in this war against us, should you even be exchanged, you are at liberty to have the freedom of the castle : otherwise I shall feel it my duty to place you in custody of the keeper of the prisons."

" I cannot accept my liberty on these conditions, senor," answered Louis.

" Nor will I!" responded Robert.

" Bueno ! Then you will be locked up. I should be happy to extend courtesy to you, senor Captain Dumont, for you have been recommended by Captain Mejia to my kindness, but as your reply shows a hostility to Mexico, I shall regard you as her enemy, as I would any other Americano : and forthwith place you in charge of the turnkey of the castle.'

"Being a prisoner, I expect, senor, only the treatment of a prisoner," answered Louis.

"Very well. Colonel Lamas! Conduct these gentlemen to their cells. Their refusal to accept parole leads me to believe that it is their intention to escape if possible; see, therefore, that they are placed in secure confinement. I shall make you, as captain of the guard, responsible for their safe custody."

The two young officers were then escorted from the hall, between two files of solders, in number, full a score, armed to the teeth, and ferocious, with formidable moustaches. They were first led from the presence of the governor into a corridor supported by massive stone pillars, where were grouped a large number of soldiers, some taking their breakfast, others smoking, others picking vermin from their clothes; and here and there in an obscure corner, one kneeling before a waxen image of the Saviour, stuck by the pressure of the thumb upon the soft wax, against the stone sides of the wall. As the two officers passed along through these groups, their ears were saluted with vindictive expressions, and the most bitter execrations against the Americanos.

"How these Mexicans hate us, Robert!" said Louis, forgetting for the moment that he spoke to an enemy, and only feeling that a common misfortune should have made them friends.

"Not more than I hate thee!" was the reply.

Louis smiled, yet that smile was exchanged the next moment for an expression of sadness, that one, otherwise noble, generous and good, should, through his hatred for him, be changed into another man altogether. Louis well knew his better nature; and, if only to restore him to himself, he would have had him his friend.

After passing along the whole length of the corridor, they were conducted through a massive gate-way into a dark passage which was faintly lighted by iron lamps placed at intervals in niches. It gradually descended, and at length was crossed at a sort of central hall or nave by various passages radicating from this point. One of these was closed by an iron door, which the guide unlocked and unbarred. It led into a narrow avenue, between damp walls. Here all the soldiers left them. As they advanced along the passage, Louis heard distinctly the dashing of the surges against the foundation of the fortress. At the extremity of the passage was a door elevated two steps from the pavement. This was unbarred and thrown open. It gave access to a room about ten feet square, lighted by a massive grated window, seven feet above the floor. On one side of the wall was a broad wooden bench, on which lay three pallets of moss. A narrower bench for a seat was opposite to it, on the other side of the wall. A stone pitcher without a handle, a bucket, and three pairs of chains fastened to huge staples in the wall constituted the only furniture of the dismal place.

"Go in, caballeros!" said the captain of the guard. "This is your prison!"

"This!" cried Robert, indignantly. "We are not felons—at least I am no murderer, or murderer's son, that I should be shut in here! Give me better quarters than these. Besides, I will not share the same cell with this man. Hell would be preferable to such a doom!"

"Have you gold, senor," significantly asked the captain.

"Yes. Give me another cell and I will pay thee fifty pesos in gold!"

"Bien!" answered the jailer; "and after locking Louis into his cell, he opened the door of one adjoining and ushered Robert into it, though taking care first to be paid the price stipulated.

CHAPTER XVII.

THE CASTLE AND THE PRISONERS.

WE now return to the two heroines of our story, Isabel Rosal and Benita, whom we left watching with the most painful suspense the engagement between the cutter and privateer.

The result of the contest was not apparent to them from the position in which they beheld it. They saw the terrific flashes of the discharged artillery, heard its loud roar, and fancied they could hear borne to their ears upon the wind the shouts and shrieks of the combatants.

At length they beheld the cutter separate from the privateer and sail up the lake, pursued for a little while by their opponent, which at length tacked and stood out towards the gulf. But they were ignorant of the character of the two vessels. At the distance the cutter was from them they could not distinguish her so as to say positively it was the vessel commanded by Louis. Their fears, however, led them to believe that it was ; and now as it approached nigher, with the loss of its fore-topmast, they were enabled to make her out to be the Ring-dove. This discovery was made by Benita with the spy-glass, and she immediately communicated the fact to Isabel, who scarcely needed this confirmation to her fears.

" Oh, that I knew his fate !" she exclaimed. " He may have fallen ! Horrid thought ?"

" Hope, lady, hope !" said Benita.

" I, I fear he has fallen : for if he was alive and on board, his courage would never have suffered him to fly, even from a superior force !"

" We shall know ere long. The cutter is standing towards us, and doubtless will come to an anchor near the shore, perhaps opposite the inlet."

They continued to watch it with deep interest as it came on. It passed the spot where they were standing, and after sailing on about a quarter of a mile, came to anchor, within three hundred yards of the shore.

" Now, Benita, take your boat, I pray you, and hasten on board," cried Isabel.

" I hope I shall bring back good news to you, lady," answered Benita, whose sympathy for Isabel almost caused her to forget that she was her rival. She was about descending to the water-side, when she beheld a boat leave the side of the cutter and pull towards the cliff, which was a well-known landing place for the adjacent region, there being a road winding round it leading to the interior. It was, therefore, nothing extraordinary, if a boat was sent ashore at all, that it should be sent to land there.

They waited for it with the utmost anxiety, Benita's quite as lively as that of Isabel ; for she loved the noble Louis with an affection that surprised even herself. But she had felt her heart draw towards him from the first moment she saw him, and without asking herself whether it were love that would issue in happiness, or sorrow, she gave her heart up to it with joy. She had found something on which to place her young affections. She loved her father, indeed ; but she yearned to love as youth ever does, some one of congenial age and feelings. Louis, to her imagination seemed created for her to love. She felt that, even though he should become the husband of Isabel, she should love him still, as ardently, as purely as now. She even loved Isabel, strange inconsistency ! fo a rival, because she loved Louis. This made Isabel dear to her—made her tender towards her, while she envied her.

The boat came nearer and nearer to the land. The maidens strained their eyes to discover the form both loved. The boat came so near that they could distinguish the features, by the moonlight, of the steersman. It was not the face of Louis.

"He is not in the boat, dear lady," sighed Benita. "But, perhaps, he has only sent it on shore. He is, no doubt, on board. Let us not fear too much."

"Us? us? Do you then feel such an interest in him?"

Before Benita could reply to this sudden inquiry, the boat struck the beach, and Ben Bulwark sprung out. Isabel at once recognised him, for she had seen him with her lover before.

"Now, my lads," said the rough voice of the seaman, "hasten up to the villa under all canvas, and ax Miss Isabel to let some o' the niggers ride off for a doctor; and see you fetch him on board. Meanwhile we'll be picking out a straight tree to cut down, and make a new top-mast out of."

"Oh, sir—oh, Mr. Bulwark, who is hurt?" cried Isabel, bounding down the path and appearing so suddenly before his face, that he started with surprise if not apprehension.

"Bless me! It is Miss Isabel! And here is a consort in tow with a spy-glass under her arm, shiver my timbers if it 'ant."

"Where is Louis—your captain? Is he hurt? You have sent a man for a doctor. Speak who needs one?"

"Four of our poor fellows who have been hit in this confounded bad affair off here."

"But your captain?" cried Benita.

"Two pretty creatures here asking me in one breath about my captain? Well I suppose I must tell you. You see we fell in with a strange sail and bore up for her. She turned out to be more than a match for us—none other than a heavy Mexican privateer. We boarded her, as our only chance of saving ourselves and capturing her, as she had the heaviest metal, but we were beat back, lost nine men and left our captain prisoner. He fought like a hero, but it was of no use. They captured him."

At this intelligence, Isabel was nearly overcome with grief. Benita forgot her own to sympathise with hers. Ben then went on to say that the cutter would refit as fast as possible, and sail in pursuit of the privateer, as Lieutenant Gladson had made oath that he would recover his captain, or perish with him."

Isabel at length became more composed. She hastened to the villa to order servants to ride for a surgeon who lived two leagues off; and at the same time she sent word to Lieutenant Gladston, that the wounded men he had mentioned must be sent on shore and placed under her charge at the villa. Gladson very willingly consented, and came ashore with the four men, as he was also slightly wounded and wanted his hurt dressed.

It was morning when the surgeon had got through his task and dismissed Gladson to the duties of getting his vessel repaired and ready to pursue the Mexican. A suitable tree was cut down, and with the aid of the slaves on the estate was soon fashioned into a mast. They were in the act of launching it into the water to tow it alongside, when a little skiff which they had been for some time watching sailing up the Cape, came so near that Benita, who was looking out anxiously to try if she could see the lugger, recognized Manuel in her.

He soon came to land, and, after embracing Benita, hurriedly asked for Isabel Rosal. He was about to go to the house when they met her coming towards the cliff; for Benita had informed her that her brother had embarked in the lugger with her father the previous night, and her anxiety about him was an additional source of grief to her.

"Senora," said old Manuel, as he come near, "I bear a message to you from Don Louis?"

"Is he safe? Does he live?" she cried between fear and hope.

"He is safe, though a prisoner. He is unharmed and well treated. I was out in my lugger with your brother——"

"And where is Robert?" she asked earnestly.

"You shall hear. We got out so far that when the engagement took place we were within range, and lingering to see the fight a shot sunk the lugger !"

"And Robert Rosal perished !" exclaimed Benita with emotion.

"No, We were a long time in the water. The cutter passed us, but was too much in a hurry to stop and pick us up. The privateer, however, hearing our shouts took us on board, for we were so many prisoners for them—and prisoners are worth money. They took master Robert and myself on board !"

"Then he is living ! Heaven be thanked !" cried Isabel.

"Yes !"

"And how is it that you have escaped, dear father ?" asked Benita, embracing him with grateful affection, and kissing again and again his bearded cheek.

"Through the kindness of Captain Louis, one of the noblest men that ever breathed."

"He is, indeed !" responded Isabel. "How is it that he is a prisoner ?"

"Because they wished to keep him, he being an officer of rank !"

Manuel then explained to them the circumstances which led to his release, and faithfully communicated every word of the message with which Louis had entrusted him.

Both of the young maidens were filled with grief at this confirmation of the capture of the brother and lover. They overwhelmed Manuel with numberless questions in reference to the probability of their escaping, of their being ransomed or being exchanged.

"I don't know how the matter will turn out," he answered. "There is no doubt that they will be well treated, and when they get to Vera Cruz, if they are not recaptured, will have their parole ! My plan would be to try and capture the Mexican ; but as there is a United States brig cruising outside, I have no doubt we could convey to her information that would result in her capture ! At any rate I am ready to offer my services to Lieutenant Gladson if he will accept them. It is true I am but one man, but then he is short-handed !"

After his interview with the two maidens, Manuel went on board the cutter and communicated to Gladson the message given him by Louis. The officer received the communication with great joy, and resolved without any but the most needful delay, to make sail out of the lake in pursuit of the brig of war.

For this purpose the preparations were so hastened that by night all was ready to make sail and start on the enterprize. But here a new matter perplexed the lieutenant as well as old Manuel. Both of the heroines of our story had resolved together that they would go with them in the cutter. As they would not hear any denial and were very positive, Gladson finally consented and gave up to them Louis' state-room, and with this addition to her force the cutter got underweigh just at sunset and stood down the lake.

The next morning they were full twenty leagues from the land ; and had run thus far without seeing anything of the U. S. brig, which Gladson hoped to fall in with. This officer now resolved to follow in the track of the privateer in the direction of Vera Cruz. Seven days afterwards, as the dawn broke on the morning after the successful entrance of the privateer into the port of Vera Cruz, the look-out cried from aloft,

"Sail ho !"

Gladson and Manuel both sprung for their spy-glasses ; but what was taken for a sail proved to be the snowy peak of one of the lofty mountains west of Vera Cruz, just emerging from the sea. They continued to sail on, and about ten o'clock a dark object was seen upon the horizon in the southern board. At first it was taken to be a ship dismasted ; but as it certainly advanced, and very rapidly too, they soon set it down for a war steamer, which, ere long, their glasses proved it to be. It continued to approach them swiftly from the south, each moment growing larger and more formidable in appearance. At length it came so near that they could see the men on her decks ; yet, as neither machinery, paddles, nor smoke were visible, she seemed to be a spirit-ship moving without the aid of the wind—nay in its very teeth. It came swiftly down upon them, passed ahead, and sailing completely round them, at length hailed and ordered them to heave to. Before this order was given Gladson had hoisted the American flag.

"What cutter is that?" demanded an officer from the steamer's deck.

"The Ringdove!" responded Gladson.

"Who commands her?"

"Captain Dumont did, sir; but his first lieutenant now."

Some further conversation passed, during which the captain of the war steamer heard of the engagement with the privateer and the capture of her captain; and Gladson heard that the privateer, or a vessel answering her description had been seen off the port, and the steamer was then in search of her. Gladson, not being able to communicate any later information touching the Mexican, was ordered to keep in the wake of the steamer and stand for the cruising ground.

It was late in the afternoon when they reached the flag-ship, where they learned that the bold privateer had got into the harbour, under cover of night, and was then in sight, anchored under the guns of the castle.

When this intelligence was communicated to Manuel by Gladson in terms of great disappointment at the result, the latter conceived an idea that it was possible to effect the escape of Louis; for the old man's bosom was alive with gratitude to the man who had purchased his ransom; and he resolved to risk his life to free him from prison. Being a Spaniard, and fluently speaking the language, he felt he could pass easily on shore as a Mexican.

He detailed his whole plan to Gladson, and also Isabel and Benita. The latter insisted on accompanying him, disguised as a young man. She said she also could be of great service to him. To this he at length consented; and it was decided that Gladson should, under the cover of night, land them on the coast, half a league from Vera Cruz; and lay off there for him. Signals were arranged, and everything planned towards a successful result to the enterprize.

The same night, therefore, about eleven o'clock, the cutter came to near the land south of the castle, landed a boat with the two adventurers, and then stood off again till the same hour the next night. Isabel sent her prayers after the disguised father and daughter, previously causing Benita to promise that she would do as much to save her brother as her lover. This Benita readily promised, both for Isabel's sake and because she had a secret regard for the young naval officer, though she loved him not with the love she had for Louis.

The two prisoners had been shut up in their adjoining cells about eighteen hours, when a plan which Louis had conceived for liberating himself was matured. He had discovered, in examining his cell, that the constant action of the sea had removed a portion of the foundation where a drain passed out under the wall, and that a huge square mass of stone had settled so far that at the flowing of the tide his cell was inundated; and through the crevice at low tide he could see the surface of the harbour.

Upon close inspection of the place, he found that by removing some pieces of rock beneath the loosened stone, it would sink still lower, and might afford him a way of escape through the passage over it. After a great deal of labour, he effected his object, and to his great joy passed through to the outside of the wall, whence, by swimming, he could reach the main land.

When he saw that escape was possible in this way, he resolved to make it the next night: but the idea of leaving Robert to his fate, was painful to him. He determined he should share his liberty with him; for having again examined the spot, he saw that by digging still lower into the sand under the rock next to that which had fallen in, the adjoining one could fall and open a way into Robert's cell. He therefore went to work, and after several hours labour, had the satisfaction of seeing the stone slide from its bed and leave a crevice into the adjacent cell, into which he could thrust his arm. He now called to Robert by name, in a suppressed whisper.

"Who is it?" demanded the prisoner, amazed.

"It is Louis. Forget for a while your hostility, dear Robert, and exert yourself to escape. I have made an opening from my cell to the outside, and partly laid open yours. With a little exertion on your part you shall be free. I am so already ; but I cannot go and leave you a prisoner with these confounded Mexicans!"

"What shall I do?" asked Robert, eagerly, as if the love of liberty was greater than his hatred.

"Remove the rubble and sand from under this larger stone and it will gradually fall on your side, as it has on this. It will take some time, but by night you will effect a passage into my cell, and so with me out underneath the walls. Do not let your dislike to me cause you to refuse this chance of escape. Once outside, we can take a boat and reach one of the fleet."

"Louis," cried Robert with emotion, "give me your hand. I cannot withstand such magnanimity. From this moment let us be brothers!"

The two young men thus suddenly reconciled, grasped hands through the opening ; and Robert immediately went to work to free himself from his prison. Just at sunset, the stone fell, and the next moment the two friends rushed into each other's arms and wept together.

"Now, Robert, let us go forth, and trust to Providence for the issue!" said Louis.

"I will follow you, Louis!"

The two young men now gained the outer side of the wall. It was low tide, and protected by the darkness, they made their way round until they came to the water-battery, where they were compelled to swim. But they had not swam far before they came to a landing, where three barges were chained ; and near them stood a sentinel. It was but the act of a moment, after noiselessly landing, to secure and gag the sentry, cast him into one of the boats, spring into it, and cast off. They now bent to their oars, with hearty good will, and pulled as they thought in the darkness, directly out of the harbour, but they mistook lights on shore for those of the fleet, and were carried by the current towards the main-land, and as the boat was large and unwieldy, they had much difficulty in managing it at all. As soon as they landed, finding they could not get to sea in the boat, they abandoned it, and struck along the beach, resolved to pursue this course, till they should fall in with some light skiff.

"Suddenly, as they passed a clump of bushes, they came upon two persons rapidly advancing towards the town. Upon seeing them they would have fled, but flight was impossible. They, therefore, stood firm, resolved to sell their lives as dearly as possible, being armed with clubs that they had picked up upon the beach.

The two men also stopped as if alarmed ; but after a moment, one advanced and boldly said in Spanish—

"Who goes there?"

"Amigos?" responded Louis. "Who are you?"

"Comoradas," answered Manuel.

"Robert, I would swear that voice was old Manuel's out of Mexico," said Louis. "At any rate they are not soldiers in search of us—we have nothing to fear."

"They seem to be fugitives as well as we."

"Amigo," said Louis, "if you are fishermen of these parts, pray sell us a boat and we will pay thee richly ?"

"It is Louis !" cried Benita, who stood by the side of Manuel. "I cannot be mistaken."

"Who calls my name ?" exclaimed Louis, with surprise.

"Are you Louis Dumont?" demanded Manuel, coming quickly forward.

"Yes and you are Manuel!"

The two men fell into each other's arms.

"And this is Master Robert," cried Manuel, embracing him. This is a Heaven's wonder brought about surely ?"

"What brought thee here, Manuel, and who is with thee?" demanded Louis.

"I came to rescue thee, if possible; and this, if the truth be told, is my daughter?"

Upon hearing this, both of the young men expressed their astonishment and pleasure, and shook her warmly by the hand.

"We have no time to lose," said Manuel. "It is not ten minutes since we left your cutter just off here round the point."

Manuel then, as he led them rapidly along, proceeded to explain the events up to this moment, and his plans for aiding their escape from prison, while from them, he heard the particulars of their reconciliation and their flight from the castle. They all regarded their meeting, as it was, as most providential. Robert and Louis were full of their protestations of thanks to Manuel and the beautiful Benita; but the latter was grieved to find that Louis talked and thought only of Isabel, to whose marriage with whom there seemed no obstacle now that Robert had for ever buried in gratitude his hostility. Robert was not, however, idle in

No. 9.

his expressions of thanks to Benita, for her part taken in the effort to bring about his escape ; and he was so warm in his thanks that she blushed at receiving them.   Having walked round the point, the cutter was now seen only a little way off.   Manuel at once made a signal by kindling a brand and whirling it in circles. It was discovered on board, and although unlooked for before the next night, it was at once obeyed, and the cutter put back, Gladson supposing Manuel had been compelled to abandon his enterprise at the outset.

Who can describe the joy of Isabel, on beholding her lover ascend the cutter's side, Robert, too, leaning on his arm.   Who can pourtray the happiness of that meeting !

It was indeed a happy reunion on board that little vessel, and the weather being fine, many hours were passed on deck, in animated conversation, and enjoyment of passing objects of interest.   Even Isabel who had been little on the great waters was very soon enchanted with the sea.   The once dreadful motion of the vessel had become a pleasure, like the breathless lift of the boy's scup, or flying in a dream. The whole day fleeted by delightfully.   Benita and Isabel generally awoke by the dawn, and lay a few moments ruminating, listening to the waves washing almost against their shoulders, or in artless and confidential revelation.   The dim lamp that burnt all night in the outer cabin, shed a faint light into their little state room. By and by the pale day beams would fall through the small thick glass—their only window—situated just above their heads. Shaking off the drowsiness of slumber, which has not been altogether interrupted by the various noises of the deck, the rolling of the ship, the change of watch, &c, and hastily clothing themselves, they would pick their steps to the companion way, and ascend to the deck.   That is equivalent to folks on land going into the parlour, or out into the street ; but what a novel and vast prospect !   In every direction spread the limitless waste of waters —heaving, dashing, breaking around.   Isabel cast a careful glance along the distant circle where the sky touches the waves,   But no whales—no leviathans—no sea serpents.   Travellers (that inventive race of beings) have peopled the deep more liberally than truth warrants.   But in one quarter of the heavens, the reddening clouds, the increasing fires, the brilliant orange, the burnished gold, the blended green and azure, and the burning glory flowing in upon the whole, and every instant becoming more and more intense, attract all waking eyes toward the pathway of the rising sun.   They watch the silent wonder which, even over the desert around, spreads cheerfulness and animation, although not that of woods, cities, flowery and vine-covered cottages.   Here the sea-birds dart about.   The wild gull wheels in the air watching his prey, unconscious while he meditates their death, that he himself is one of the most soft-looking and graceful creatures in existence.   And other wild birds are fluttering and circling about, ever dipping their little bills in the water.   Sometimes a huge porpoise rolls heavily over with a splash and a snort ; and occasionally the rosy beams of day are reflected from a sail stealing along the extreme line of prospect, and shining like a star.   By this time other folks mount the deck besides our two heroines, the silent man at the helm and his assistant watch.   The steward and mates appear at their various vocations. The vessel presents a multiplicity of seats—cushions of old sail—coils of rope— piles of timber—and upon one of these they fling themselves down with the perfect enjoyment of a holiday.

Then came the summons to breakfast, and the meeting with their friends ; the meal is prolonged with social chat, but even the happiest breakfast will end.   The sky now becomes soft and warm.   The few visible clouds lie in motionless groups. The breeze freshens as the day advances.   The leaning vessel cleaves the flood, and they foam merrily on their course.   The lovers may walk the deck now without interruption, except an occasional cry of " sail, ho !" or the words of the helmsman, " four bells," or the voice of the captain, " how d'ye hea'd ?" or, " keep her full," or some casual remark from a passing companion.   Time flies till the steward summons to dinner.   With the aid of reading, talking and laughing, the afternoon glides just as pleasantly by, enlivened by numerous little incidents which could only happen on the ocean, and thus, day after day, melted into the past. If the sea and weather were always thus, who would not spend his time upon it. But the beauty of the season was almost unparalleled.

Then the sunsets! We may fling by the pallet in despair. We shall not enter upon the philosophy of ocean sunsets, nor examine whether their peculiarities arise from the purity of the atmosphere or the absence of land-exhalations; but certainly they are the most enchanting exhibitions to which nature ever admitted mere mortals :

> ————"Inimitable on earth,
> By model or by shaded pencil drawn."

Their majestic and solemn glory hushes us to silence, and we enjoy them more as the tokens of a " goodly day to-morrow." The departure of the sun from the heavens is everywhere a glorious spectacle, not unmingled with sadness. To the commonest comprehension, it presents a striking and mournful emblem. It is disappointment. It is farewell. It is death. Love, glory, hope, ambition, pause before the last splendours of the dying god, as he sinks into the darkness which must wrap all human things. Only a devout man can look upon it without a sigh or a shudder.

But it is not merely for its poetic associations, nor its inexpressiable magnifience, that we never could resist the influence of the setting sun, for it displays much more than we can gather through the mere corporeal vision. We see not only a narrow orb passing beneath the horizon, and painting the heavens with radiant light; but we behold a globe of inconceivably stupendous dimensions, a million times larger than the earth—composed of matter unknown to science, having for ages deluged immensity with inexhaustible floods of glory, and from which the surface where we stand is receding at the rate of one thousand miles an hour. When the disk is upon the horizon, this tremendous and solemn motion is perceptible to human eyes, and fills and overwhelms the mind with ideas of vastness and sublimity.

The ocean is wonderful and divine in its forms and changes and sounds, in its grandeur, its beauty, its inhabitants, its uses, and its mysteries, its variety; in all that strikes the sense and is immediately apprehended by the understanding. But besides all these, and lying deeper than all, it possesses a moral interest, which is partly bestowed upon it, and partly borrowed from it, by the mind of man. The soul finds in it a fund of high spiritual associations. Analogies are perceived in it, which connect it most affectingly with our mortal life, with dread eternity, and with Almighty God himself, the source and end of all. And thus it becomes a principal link in that great chain of purpose and sympathy, wiih which the Creator has bound up all matter and mind, together with his own infinite being, in one concentrating whole.

The sea has often been likened to this our life. Poetry is fond of remarking resemblances between it and the passions and fortunes of humanity. Our contemplations launch forth on its capacious bosom, and gather up the images and shadowings of our existence and fate, of what we are, and what is appointed to us. Do we see its multitudinous waves rushing blindly and impetuously along whenever they are driven by the lashing wind? They remind us of the tempest of an angry mind, or the tumult of an enraged people. Are the waves hushed, and is a calm breathed over the floods? It is the similitude of a peaceful breast, of a composed and placid spirit, or a quiet, untroubled time. Doubts, anxieties, and fears pass over our minds, as clouds do over the sea, tinging them, as the clouds tinge the waters, with their deep and threatening hues. Does a beaming hope or a golden joy break in suddenly upon us, in the midst of care or misfortune? What is it but a ray of light, such as we sometimes behold sent down from the rifted sky, shining alone in the dark horizon, a sun-burst on a sullen sea? But we must leave philosophy, and proceed with the story.

The charming and faithful Benita finding that Louis Dumont was wholly lost in the love of Isabel, sighed and listened, as the cutter sailed homewards, in many a starry walk on deck to the deep passion of Robert Rosal ; and at length made him happy by the confession of a reciprocal love ; though such love as Louis had awakened in her bosom she could not feel, he had not the power to kindle; for that love was lighted by the torch of nature, and even when some weeks afterwards, Louis had become the bridegroom of Isabel, and she the bride of Robert, it was not extinguished, nay, but burned with a holier, purer flame, yet without passion or madness—for Louis was her brother.

This was the secret of her love. She mistook the natural affection of a sister for the deeper, wilder love of the soul.

Manuel unfolded this secret. He saw on board that Benita loved Louis, and was wasting for love of him. He, therefore, the evening before they re-entered Lake Borgne, told them as they were all assembled together, how he had saved the little girl, who had been carried away by the current and supposed to be drowned; and loving the child, and being alone and solitary, he had kept the secret, and brought it up as his own.

"Yet you shall ever be my father—Benita will ever be thy child," were her fervent words in his glad ear, as she threw herself, in tears of wonder and joy, first upon his shoulder. She then cast herself upon Louis's bosom, from which, so overflowing with joy was the young heart, she was removed by Robert almost insensible; but she was soon enabled to realize, with deep gratitude and sweet peace, the happiness that had been vouchsafed to her.